DOLCE VITA
MURDERS

DOLCE VITA MURDERS

DI Jellicoe Book Four

Jack Murray

Books by Jack Murray

DI Jellicoe Series
A Time to Kill
The Bus Stop
Trio
Dolce Vita Murders

Kit Aston Series
The Affair of the Christmas Card Killer
The Chess Board Murders
The Phantom
The Frisco Falcon
The Medium Murders
The Bluebeard Club
The Tangier Tajine
The Empire Theatre Murders (May 2023)
The French Diplomat Affair (novella)
Haymaker's Last Fight (novelette)

Agatha Aston Series
Black-Eyed Nick
The Witchfinder General Murders
The Christmas Murder Mystery

Danny Shaw / Manfred Brehme WWII Series
The Shadow of War)
Crusader
El Alamein

ISBN: 9798372686601
Imprint: Independently published

For my Monica, Lavinia, Anne and our angel baby, Edward...

Prologue

Somewhere nr Palermo, Sicily: May 1949

Felix M. Scheffler fixed his eyes on the man in front of him. As much as he tried, it was impossible to feel neutral about the man he faced. It was neither hate nor respect. Nor was it fear or disdain. Salvatore Lucania was not a man who provoked disinterestedness in people; it was usually fear. He'd changed his name many years before after coming to America. The name that he'd chosen would make him infamous: Charles Luciano. They called him 'Lucky' and perhaps he was, but the man Scheffler was gazing at did not strike him as someone who relied on good fortune.

What was he doing here? Seated in front of him was a man feared in Italy and in America. A man who had been a gang boss, Il Capo, in his home country. He was responsible for the death of dozens of men in the gang wars in Chicago during the thirties until he'd been imprisoned. If that had been the story then Felix M. Scheffler, he'd been advised to keep the 'M' by a lawyer friend, would not be in Sicily, in a tiny house on a nondescript street in Palermo. Yet this was not 'Lucky' Luciano's story. Not by a long shot.

During the war, at the request of President Roosevelt no less, a commie in Scheffler's book but no matter, Luciano had been instrumental in bringing together the various clans on the island of Sicily to oppose the German occupation and thus facilitate the invasion of the island in 1943. How many men had Luciano been responsible for killing? Probably dozens, maybe hundreds. Yet how many men, American fighting men, had been saved by his intervention on the island? Tens of thousands was at the lower end of any estimate. The man was a hero in many ways.

And yet.

So here he was at Uncle Sam's behest, Albert Scheffler's boy, a senior operative for the Central Intelligence Agency in Europe having to parlay with a known gangster who was still up to his heavy-lidded eyes in organised crime. It would have made him sick to the pit of his stomach if he thought about it too much. Imagine, Uncle Sam would turn a blind eye to Luciano's activities in Europe; it would ignore the French Connection whereby drugs would flow into France from Indochina before surging like a tidal wave around the rest of Europe. All because Uncle Sam feared an even greater enemy than the young, the rich and the feckless of Europe becoming hooked on heroin or cocaine or marijuana.

They feared Communism.

This was the real enemy. The threat posed by the enemy within as well as from the east was undeniable. If there was any morality that Scheffler could mine from the filth around him then it was this. Scheffler was not stupid. He was making a deal with the devil, but, men like him were born to perform this role. What separated him from normal men was not his patriotism, even Scheffler recognised that this was a cheap purchase, no, it was his willingness to put this sense of duty on the line, to navigate between the black and the white, between good and evil to reach a place where morality could flourish untainted. In other words he was not so much laying down his life as his soul for the cause that mean most to him: freedom.

'You want me to kill Roggero Riva,' said Luciano.

This was not quite how Scheffler had put it. His words were couched around removing a problem. Looking into the eyes of the shark before him, Scheffler realised that to make such a distinction for a man like Luciano would, quite rightly, be perceived as weakness. He would not look weak in front of this man.

'Yes, Mr Luciano. The Agency wants you to kill him. The people on this island must know that Communism will not be welcomed by my country. A country that you and I both know, Mr Luciano, is keeping not just Italy but the whole of Europe from starvation, destitution and let's be honest here, Stalin and all that implies.

Scheffler felt a surge of power flowing through his body. His dad would be so proud. To gaze unblinking into the eyes of a man feared by everyone on this island and tell him, yes, tell him what he must do was to experience a feeling of elation that he could not quite remember feeling before.

Luciano nodded and stood up from the table.

'Deal.'

He turned away from the CIA man and walked out of the room. The sound of the door closing was like a pin popping his inflated sense of achievement. He had been dismissed. He, Felix M. Scheffler had been dismissed by a two-bit hoodlum. He felt like shouting at the gangster. Then he looked into the eyes of the two men standing either side of the door. What he saw were dark pools where the light of morality or doubt would never shine.

Perhaps not.

*

Filippo Vitale and Olivio Randazzo strolled along the edge of the cliff utterly impervious to the drop below them. If either of them felt any nervousness about what they had been asked to do then neither would show it. They were not frightened virgins fumbling around in the dark. They had done bad things before. This was why Il Capo trusted them. They did as they were told. This is how they had been brought up. You learn more from your father's hand than you do at school. Everyone knew this, eventually.

Even when Il Capo asked them to wear masks they had not blanched. There was not so much as a muscle twitching on their face when he asked them to do something they would normally recoil from doing, but Il Capo understood this. They could hear it in his voice. They were doing this for their benefactor: the United States of America. God bless America, they'd said, when they were leaving the little house where Il Capo lived. How they'd laughed.

'I don't like America telling us what we can do,' said Vitale. 'Who the hell do they think they are?'

'Our bankers, Filippo, and don't forget, Capo is American now. He'll look after us.'

'Did you see the look on the CIA man's face when he left the room?'

'He put him in his place,' agreed Randazzo.

They cut in land away from the coast.

'Where does he work again?'

'He's a butcher. Owns a shop.'

'And him a Communist. Do you think he shares his profits with the community?' asked Vitale in a mocking tone.

'Does he hell,' came the response.

They were nearing the town now. The two men put scarves around the lower part of their faces. They were already wearing caps so very little of their faces could be seen.

'I don't know why all of the teams agreed to let Torino win the league,' said Randazzo presently, changing the subject perhaps to hide any latent nervousness. 'It's not their fault the plane crashed.' He was referring to the plane crash a week earlier in which an entire football team had died. They were currently leading the race for the title. As a mark of respect the other teams in the league agreed to end the title race there and then and allow Torino to be crowned champions.

'You don't think it was deliberate?' asked Vitale.

'I hadn't thought of that,' said Randazzo. 'It's a thought isn't it?' He pointed to the main street where there was a butchers shop midway. Vitale nodded. This was the shop they had been told to visit. Each man put his hand in his pocket and felt the reassuring cold steel.

*

He wielded the knife like a surgeon's scalpel. He was in his early twenties, not especially tall or good-looking. His deep-set eyes suggested intelligence but this was not essential for his job. He looked down at his hands. They were red raw from the cold of the room in which he was butchering the meat. All around him were the carcasses of animals: cows, wild boar, chickens. The knife he wielded was sharp enough to slice through concrete. It had been his father's knife and before that, his late grandfather's. In the front he heard his father chatting with one of the regulars to their shop. He heard the same

5

conversation a dozen times a day. It was usually one-sided, his father ranting against the De Gaspieri government. His latest hobbyhorse was the proposal to join NATO.

His second hobbyhorse was his hatred of the Communist leader Togliatti because he had sat back and allowed all of this to happen just so that he could get his hands on the reins of power. He was no more than a poodle claimed the young man's father, Roggero Riva. The customer may have agreed or disagreed but he or she was certainly not going to get a word in either way.

Silence fell eventually which suggested that the customer had either been served or expired through boredom. This made the young man smile. He adored his father but sometimes he could be a little fanatical. He continued sawing the joint when he looked up. His father appeared in the opening. A beaded net separated the shop from the backroom where the young man was busy. His father smiled at his son. The young man smiled back. Then they both heard a bell ring. The door of the shop had opened.

His father turned around. Two shots were fired in such close proximity to one another that the young man guessed it had to be two guns. His father was blown into the backroom from the force of the bullets. He fell to the ground.

Dead.

Still clutching the knife, the young man raced over to his father. His worst fears were confirmed. Rage ripped through his body like an inferno. He raced through the opening out into the shop. From somewhere in the back he heard his mother asking what was going on.

*

Three days later in the house used by Charles 'Lucky' Luciano, the young man appeared in the front room. His face was almost unrecognisable; his nose had been broken, one eye was almost shut and the other soon would be. These were just the injuries Luciano could see. He suspected there would be a few broken ribs and his love life would take a while to recover.

The young man was only just about able to make out the man he knew only as Il Capo. Everyone on the island knew who this man was. Luciano nodded and the two men either side of the young man released him. He fell to the floor with a groan.

Luciano did not move from his seat. He waited a minute for the young man to get to his feet. The only sound in the room was that of the young man's laboured breathing. The young man and Luciano's eyes met. The American gangster could feel the hatred pouring from the young man. It was almost like a separate presence in the room. He had no doubt that if the two other men were not there, the young man, despite his injuries, would attempt to tear him limb from limb. The thought was oddly comforting.

'You killed my men,' said Luciano simply.

'I filleted them,' slurred the young man from a jaw that might have been broken and teeth that certainly were. 'I filleted them like the animals they were.'

'You'd kill me too if you had the chance, wouldn't you?' said Luciano. There was a half-smile on his face.

'I will kill you,' replied the young man and Luciano knew he meant it.

'No, you won't,' said Luciano simply. 'Blood for blood. You've killed two of my men. As it was your father that was

7

killed, I think that makes us even. Blood for blood. Do you understand?'

Luciano didn't wait for an answer. He opened a drawer of the table he was sitting by. From it he pulled a large knife. It was the young man's knife. Luciano inspected it appreciatively. He ran his fingers along the sharp line and whistled.

'You can do a lot of damage with this,' he mused. Then, without warning, he slammed the pointed end into the table. 'Leave us,' he said to the two men. They hesitated. Luciano was of the school that believed if an instruction was not obeyed immediately or understood then one simply needed to repeat it at the top of your voice. People usually heard then. 'Leave us,' he screamed.

The young man stared from the knife to Luciano and then back to the knife.

'Take it,' said Luciano. His voice was almost kindly. 'It's yours. Go on. Take it.'

The young man stepped forward and tried to pull the knife out with his right hand. It wouldn't move. He tried both hands. After a few seconds he was able to pull it out. He held it in his hand now and stared at Luciano. There was a frown on his face.

'Go on. You said you would kill me. Go on, then. What are you waiting for?'

Indeed, what was he waiting for? The young man considered his options. Despite his injuries, he could easily kill the man before him such was his expertise with the knife. It would be over in seconds, but what if Il Capo had a gun? He couldn't see the gangster's hands and what would happen to him when he'd killed the man who was viewed as a hero on the island? A King. Then there was his mother and sister. What

8

would happen to them? They would die. No question about it. All of these thoughts went through his head in the blink of an eye.

Luciano nodded at the young man. He liked what he saw. Despite his youth he was weighing his options. Luciano could read the calculus in the young man's eyes. Many his age would have instantly tried to exact their revenge. It would have been the last thing they ever did.

'Good choice,' said Luciano putting his left hand on the table. He was holding a gun. He set the gun down and leaned forward. His voice was low, but it still managed to chill the young man, throwing water over the fiery hatred within him.

'I'll look after you, son. I'll look after you and your family, but you work for me now.'

1

Nine years later:

London: 2nd August 1958

The argument had been loud, long and bitter. As usual. She stared at the man in front of her with tears in her eyes. The baby was crying. It was a sound that never ceased from early in the morning until exhaustion carried her away beyond the desolation of her life into a dreamless sleep.

'Can't you make that damn kid shut up?' snarled the man. He was clutching a bottle of beer. Flecks of spittle flew from his mouth. 'If you can't, I will.'

What had she been thinking making this man her lover? Was it his money? It certainly hadn't been his manner. The arrogance that had first attracted her, repelled her now. More than this it scared her. She no longer sensed the violence within him, she experienced it now. The slaps were more frequent. When would his open hand become a fist? When would he use it on their baby?

'Don't you dare, Joe, so help me I'll...'

He stepped forward menacingly.

'You'll what?' he sneered.

This quietened her but it was too late. Moments later she was reeling to the ground following the slap. This time it had been with the back of his hand. She'd felt the knuckles rip into her cheek. She was scared now.

He stepped forward and placed the bottle on the table. Putting his hands on both knees he crouched and stared down at her.

'Not so full of yourself now, are you Suze?' he whispered. The tone chilled her. It seemed he would be capable of anything at that moment. The baby's crying grew in pitch and intensity. Joe swore and turned to the baby. He rose up and began to stumble in the direction of the cot.

'Don't touch Billy,' shouted the young woman. There was no hiding the note of hysteria in her voice. 'Don't you dare touch him.'

But Joe ignored her. He moved forward towards the cot until he was standing over it.

'Will you shut your mouth he roared,' at the crying child. 'So help me, I'll...'

Whatever he had intended saying was lost at that moment. He collapsed to the ground. Standing over him was Susan. She was clutching the bottle he'd left on the table. She stared in horror at what she'd done. A blood-red halo formed around Joe's head. Panic gripped her. She picked up the baby from the cot and held him closely.

'Don't worry, Billy. It'll be all right. Just you see.'

Then the body on the floor began to stir. She heard a moan. She had to leave. Get away. Far away. She had to do it now. There were places she could go. Her friends had told her. That was it. She'd go to the shelters. They'd look after her. Joe would never see her or the baby again. She glanced towards the pram. Moments later the baby was in the pram and Susan was grabbing money from a jar. She turned to see Joe. He was still on the ground, but he was moving his legs.

It was now or never. There was no time for her things. She had money. She had her bag. Most of all, she had Billy.

She left.

*

The argument had been loud, long and bitter. As usual. It seemed to Jellicoe they were becoming more frequent, more fatiguing, more futile. What was the point now? By arguing with Sylvia he was becoming complicit in her affairs. To quarrel implied an acceptance of a premise that was intolerable. Yet he had put up with it. The reason why was not hard to fathom. Jellicoe looked around at their beautiful flat. He was living in a type of luxury that most policemen could only dream about. Such a place was beyond the wage of all but the most senior of policemen.

The door slammed shut causing Jellicoe to spin around. He stood for second unsure what to do. Follow her? Plead with her to come back? Take what dignity he had left and throw it on the ground then stamp on it for good measure?

No.

There was a limit to this, and Jellicoe was fast reaching it. Anger flared in his eyes. Without thinking he strode towards the door that Sylvia had left through. He yanked it open and ran down the corridor to the entrance hallway. He saw Sylvia up ahead at the front entrance. She nodded to the doorman, George, as she passed. George raised a finger in the air and then Jellicoe saw a taxi pull up outside the apartment block.

For a moment Jellicoe's heart stopped beating. A moment of realisation. She was beautiful, rich and so much smarter than

12

he. What was he doing? Her slim figure was silhouetted in the doorway. She skipped gracefully down the steps towards the waiting taxi. Energy surged through him.

'Sylvia,' he shouted. There was enough anger in his voice to make George turn and look at him from the other side of the glass doors.

If Sylvia had heard him, she was certainly not going to acknowledge it. She walked forward, eyes ahead, ignoring the looks of the men on the street. She had seen these looks since she was twelve years old. They had scared her then, now they bored her. She understood what they wanted. So obvious, so ridiculous, so funny. Sometimes.

Was Nick following her? It would be a first. Normally, he would stare sullenly at her. They would not speak for a day.

Then...

She almost felt sorry for him. Their marriage was sham. While it had not always been so, it was now. This made her feel neither happy nor sad. There had been wonderful moments over the last few years but just as many low points too. She couldn't blame him really. There was no question where the fault lay except, perhaps, for one thing: he should never have married her. She had beguiled him, and, for a time, his good looks had entranced her too. He had a movie star quality to him that he did not realise. This made him all the more attractive. It's often the things we do not realise about ourselves that attract or repel people. Perhaps not knowing is best. We should kiss beauty as it flies, as the poet said.

But looks are not everything. He'd found that out the hard way. Schopenhauer, a favourite writer of Jellicoe's, was right: his passion for Sylvia's beauty blinded him to her faults, and his too, which made them two people who would never have made good friends never mind a married couple.

She walked towards the taxi and felt just a slight twinge that might have been regret had she thought about it long enough. He'd done nothing wrong, really. In fact, more than this, at a certain point, he had been the right one, but it was all coming to an end now. Everything. She no longer needed him. Freedom beckoned. A divorce was not the end of the world. She was not yet twenty-six. There would be time to enjoy herself once more before settling down. She would do what her father wanted. Before that it would be her turn. It was going to be fun.

She stepped inside the black taxi, gleaming in the late afternoon sunshine.

'Where to, miss?' said the driver. A real Londoner's voice. He could have been wearing a black suit adorned with pearls on his way to central casting. For a moment she imagined him singing 'Knee's up Mother Brown'.

A voice outside was shouting. It was shouting to her. She heard her name. It was Nick. He sounded different. Gone was the sense of hurt that she knew so well. Gone was the hint of appeal. In its place was anger. No question. He was raging. The animalistic snarl as he called her name was unmistakeable. Almost tangible. She heard a baby crying.

Jellicoe saw the taxi. A mother passed him pushing a pram. She was running but slowed momentarily. The woman glared at Jellicoe angrily but rushed on. She went to cross the road as traffic came to a halt.

Inside the taxi, Sylvia turned away and answered the driver, 'The Savoy, please.'

The taxi driver's eyes shot up to the rear-view mirror. Her voice had felt like a gentle kiss on the cheek. He saw a young woman in her twenties, dark hair, dark eyes with just a hint of olive skin. You didn't see women like this in Peckham where he lived.

Someone was shouting. It sounded like 'Sylvia'. She looked up and caught his eye. He looked away. He thought he saw a slight crinkle as she smiled.

The shouting was louder now. Sylvia turned to look out of the window at her husband. She was right. There was genuine fury in his eyes. George the doorman was looking on with concern in his eyes. Then Jellicoe started moving towards her. His eyes were fixed on hers.

'Can you hurry?' said Sylvia to the driver, not taking her eyes away from her husband.

The taxi driver glanced at his rear wing mirror. There was traffic. A lot of it.

'Come on,' he murmured.

The passenger door opened just as the driver saw a woman up ahead almost get knocked down as she tried to dodge through the traffic with a pram. She'd been looking in the wrong way; probably in the direction of the shouting.

'Silly bint, and with a child too,' said the driver.

The taxi door opened. Something felt wrong. Sylvia looked up sharply. A man had opened the taxi door. She was about to point out that he taxi was taken when she saw it. He was holding something. It glinted in the light suffusing the interior of the cab. Confused she stared open-mouthed. The scream died on her lips.

Jellicoe ran towards the taxi screaming angrily at his wife. She had looked away from him which angered him all the more.

He yanked open the door to the taxi and stared inside at his wife.

⬚

2

One year later:

London: 11th August 1959

Taranjit Shindi was proud of his name. In Punjabi, Taranjit meant "victory over bondage". The young Taranjit interpreted this as a call to represent the poor, the oppressed, the forgotten. A practical boy also, he felt that this was best achieved through the agency of practicing law. He wanted to be like his hero, Mahatma Gandhi, and so a lawyer he became. Fifty years later, he had a successful practice in the world's capital city, in his not so humble opinion, London.

When he took on clients he did not need to explain his name. For Sikhs in London, he was the automatic choice to be their legal representative, to fight their cause in England, to overcome the injustice they invariably faced. He had few non-Indian clients but when he did so, he made it a point to explain the etymology of his name.

In the year of our Lord, 1959, he had but two non-Indian clients remaining. Nick Jellicoe had been with him for five years. Taranjit had seen him though the purchase of two flats, one marriage and, sadly, one death which led to the inquest he was now attending. When he had first explained the meaning of his name, Jellicoe had frowned slightly, his gaze had intensified momentarily and then he nodded.

He had not laughed.

How many non-Indian clients had he lost because of the offence he'd taken at their low amusement of the meaning of Taranjit? Not many, true, but then again, he had never had many English clients. This bothered Taranjit more than he would admit. He was a not just a good lawyer, he was an outstanding one. A talent such as his should have been able to command the greatest clients in the kingdom. Yet his name, his colour and his race made him an outsider. All the more reason why he would have valued Nick Jellicoe had he not also developed a liking for the young man and his family. Taranjit could not help himself in this regard. He had to like his clients too otherwise any victory was hollow, robbed of its glory.

He won often.

Taranjit sat alongside his other remaining client James Jellicoe, the father of Nick. Beside Jellicoe's father was a slender woman in her late forties. She was formidable of aspect, angry by disposition and she was as Irish as the Book of Kells. She was Jellicoe's mother. They gazed at the young man pacing back and forth like a caged lion. Taranjit, himself, resembled nothing more than a stationary steam engine as he puffed smoke from his never-ending supply of cigars. Nick had declined the offer of one despite Taranjit's promise that it would help take his mind off the imminent verdict from the inquest. The father, his features drawn tighter than a bow string had accepted a cigar. He started smoking before Taranjit had lit it. It seemed the father was even more nervous than the son.

'Sit down,' said Taranjit to Jellicoe the younger. 'You're wearing a hole in the carpet.'

'He's wearing a hole in my nerves,' added James Jellicoe irritably.

Jellicoe stopped and stared at the two men. His father was dressed in his Assistant Chief Constable's uniform. This was against the advice of other senior officers who had told him it would not reflect well on the force if his son was found to have a case to answer over the death of his wife. The photographers would have field day with the two men standing together, one in uniform.

James Jellicoe's response to this advice had been brutally short but enormously satisfying. He had no doubt of his son's innocence. Moreover, he was aghast that this had not been established a year ago when they had lost Sylvia. Damn poor police work in his view and it was one he had shared frequently and loudly with anyone who would listen, and now, finally, they were almost in the clear. Even the semi-competent fatheads running the inquest could not avoid drawing a line under an inquiry that should never have happened.

Or could they...?

James Jellicoe did not want to think about it. No one possessing even a modicum of intelligence could possibly find against his son. When the woman with the baby came forward it surely must have wiped away all doubt in the small minds of the sceptics, the doubters and the congenitally stupid.

Jellicoe resumed his pacing in front of the window while Taranjit puffed contentedly on his cigar. The eyes of the lawyer roved upwards to the ceiling stained by the smoke of a thousand cigarettes. How many others had sat here while they were sitting waiting to hear the verdict of a case that might change their lives forever? In Taranjit's mind this would only change Jellicoe's life for the better, and in more ways than he could imagine.

The inquest was over, and it was, in his view, a clear victory. From this other things would arise, and he, Taranjit, would make sure that Jellicoe got what he deserved. He stretched his legs out and put his hands behind his head as he contemplated the future. This wasn't just an attempt to communicate confidence to his client; this was a typical pose. He liked nothing better than to greet clients with his feet up on the desk and his hands behind his head. He'd seen a movie where a Hollywood producer had done something similar. It was a visual communication of many things: power, confidence and, importantly, a sense that he had already won.

'Nick, my friend, please sit down. You have no case to answer. Really,' said Taranjit.

Jellicoe stopped once more and hoped he was right. It was easy for Taranjit to say. Tomorrow, the lawyer would still have his life, his career, his next case. Not Jellicoe. All this would end, whatever happened at trial.

'We'll see,' said Jellicoe. 'I'm not sure Ed Ross will ever agree.'

'Do you want me and some Sikhs to go round to his house with some hockey sticks?'

This seemed to wake Jellicoe's father up from his reverie. He jerked around and said to him, 'Really Taranjit. Someone might hear you.'

'I'm with Taranjit,' said Mrs Eileen Jellicoe. 'Pandora's box will be a dinner party compared to what I'll rain down on them.' The accent was of Dublin, part lilt, part threat with just a thread of humour running through everything that was said.

'Is that the sound of the wooden spoon being removed from the drawer?' asked Jellicoe, a warm grin spreading over his face.

'I'll take the spoon to you, ya little bollocks,' replied Mrs Jellicoe.

Taranjit shrugged unapologetically, a grin splitting his face. Even Jellicoe had to smile at the little lawyer.

He wondered if Stephen or Claudia Temple, Sylvia's parents, would show up for the verdict. They had only attended one day of the inquest. Neither had acknowledged him. He couldn't blame them for this. It was their daughter after all who had been murdered. Why should they say "good morning" to a man that was suspected of murdering her? They had never really liked him yet, at the same time, he did not believe they thought him a killer. Over the last year since Sylvia's death, contact had been infrequent, perfunctory and had effectively stopped six months ago without much sense of regret on either side.

Any further thoughts on this were interrupted by a knock on the door. A big, uniformed policeman entered. He saluted Jellicoe's father.

'I think they're ready to announce the verdict, sir.'

Jellicoe exchanged a glance with his father. James Jellicoe tried to smile in encouragement but gave it up as a bad job. He threw the remains of the cigar into a small basket by the chair. Then the three men trooped silently down a corridor into a large conference room.

'Are you coming?' asked Jellicoe to his mother who had remained seated. She shook her head. There were tears forming in her eyes. He smiled to her but could think of nothing to say. He turned and walked into the conference room.

As soon as he entered the room he saw Claudia Temple, Sylvia's mother. There was no sign of Stephen. She ignored him, staring stonily out of the window, smoking a cigarette. Jellicoe glanced at her hand. It was shaking a little. She stubbed out the cigarette and lit another with a silver lighter that Sylvia had bought her for her birthday.

Sitting across from them was his Superintendent, Ian Frankie. His lips were pursed but, then again, they usually were. He looked like he'd just received some gossip of which he thoroughly disapproved. Beside him was Superintendent Mick Lester from Scotland Yard. Nominally, he was leading the investigation into the "black cab murders", but he was a year or less away from retirement. He had fall guy written all over his hang dog features. Beside him was Chief Inspector Colin Grout. Jellicoe liked him. He was a pro. Win or lose he would take no joy from the process that he had followed. This was not the case with the other investigating officer, Detective Inspector Ed Ross. Ross and Jellicoe had joined around the same time and had enjoyed similarly rapid progress through the ranks. Ross scowled at Jellicoe as he saw him enter the room.

Jellicoe took this as a good sign.

There was no sign of Jellicoe's Chief Inspector, Reg Burnett. Clearly it had been decided that only Superintendent Frankie would appear. Jellicoe, Taranjit and his father took their seats as the head of the inquest, Sir Spiers Campbell, looked up from a sheaf of papers he was holding. Campbell was all military moustache and luxuriant eyebrows.

'Gentlemen,' he intoned sombrely in the manner of a man who was intent in extracting every last ounce of hope from the room and replacing it with a sense of his great dignity. This was his first high-profile inquest, and he was going to prolong the experience for as long as he could. Jellicoe felt his heart lurch. There was no hint of reassurance in the morose Scotsman's face. There was nothing but dignified loathing.

This was not such a good sign.

*

An hour earlier, Stephen Temple sat staring out of his apartment window overlooking Regent's Park. Apartment hardly did justice to the enormous residence. His seat was behind a large oak desk in a room with books that adorned shelves that rose to a high ceiling. A chandelier that would not have been out of place at Versailles was suspended perilously in the middle of the room. Temple always made a point of walking around it. If it were down to him then it would have been replaced years ago. As it was, the money to afford such a luxurious pied a terre in London as well as a pile in the country was as much down to his wife's wealth as his.

He turned as he saw Claudia enter. She was dressed in black, a futile piece of symbolism to remind the inquest of why they were sitting and what she had lost. What they had both lost. The thought of Sylvia caused a wave of sadness to engulf him.

'Are you coming?' she asked in that beautifully modulated voice that only hinted at her Italian origins. She had been brought up by English nannies in Rome. It showed in her accent: upper crust English yet not quite, just better.

'I think not,' replied Temple. He couldn't bear to go. It would only bring all of the pain back. Yet did he not want that also? Why else would he have the beautiful photograph of his daughter facing him on the desk. It was there as his penance. This would be formally, if implicitly, acknowledged soon at the inquest. Then the investigation would begin. He would help it in the only way that he could.

'You think it's a foregone conclusion,' said Claudia. There was no rise in inflection at the end to make this a question. It was a statement of fact.

Stephen Temple nodded absently. It would have been so much better had they found Jellicoe guilty. It would have given him something to focus on. All his guilt would have been excised then transformed into hatred; concentrated on one thing. Nick Jellicoe.

'Phone me, darling, once you know,' said Temple.

Claudia nodded and then left him alone. He returned once more to surveying Regent's Park. Soon the people in the park became blurred by the tears in his eyes. How long he stayed this way he knew not. The trance was only broken by the shattering shrillness of the telephone on his desk.

He stared at the phone for a moment not daring to pick it up. Then his hand moved reluctantly towards it and lifted it slowly up like it was an unexploded bomb. He placed the phone to his ear. He listened for a few moments then he said, 'Thank you my dear. I'll see you soon.'

The phone was dropped back into place. His head was spinning now, and he could hardly breathe. He shut his eyes to ease the pounding in his temple. It didn't work. He opened his eyes once more and looked down at the drawers in his desk. The brass handles glinted in the light. He pulled open the middle drawer. A silver-coloured object lay there also glinting.

Underneath was a photograph. He took out the photograph and looked at it.

There were half a dozen people sitting at a table in a night club. Five men including himself and Sylvia. In one hand was a cigarette, in the other, a glass of champagne. She was laughing at a joke. Her whole eyes sparkled with youth and vivacity making the diamond broach seem recessive by comparison. Her whole life lay ahead of her at that point. Yet only a few months later she was dead.

One of the men had his arm around Sylvia. He was laughing too. Temple couldn't remember the joke. It couldn't have been so funny as he was not laughing or perhaps he'd not understood. His Italian was still rather rudimentary. Sylvia had been taught by her mother and was bi-lingual. He set the photograph down on the desk in front of him and returned his gaze to the metal object in the drawer.

He reached inside and took it in his hand. Despite its heft it felt light, and cold, and deadly.

3

London: 17th August 1959

'Surely now you'll try one?' asked Taranjit holding out one of his cigars.

He was speaking to Jellicoe on the steps of Dinsdale, Dinsdale and Charlton, a legal firm near Chancery Lane. It had been a week since the verdict which had cleared Jellicoe of any wrongdoing and reinstated his right to work as a policeman. Frankie had been surprisingly generous in his reaction. Perhaps it was relief that he had not had a 'wrong 'un' in his police force, perhaps also he was concerned that the verdict might persuade Jellicoe to return to London which would leave him undermanned. Thankfully, the superintendent's insatiable desire for the limelight meant that he and Taranjit happily answered reporters' questions immediately afterwards. Frankie had suggested he take a couple of weeks off and then return to work. It would come out of his holiday allowance of course.

They heard the news an hour later.

Stephen Temple had killed himself. The details only became apparent as the week wore on. Claudia had called him to reveal the result of the inquest. As the papers' said, the poor man, still in the depths of his grief had taken his own life. It made sense and the narrative was established.

Only Jellicoe was not buying it. His senses were telling him there was another story at play. Then there was the message from Claudia asking him to come to the apartment after they had seen the lawyers. Jellicoe felt Taranjit clapping him on the back.

'You're a rich man now, Nick. You have choices that few men have these days. We need to chat about what you will do with the money. You need to invest it of course. Keep some aside for enjoying yourself but don't overdo it,' warned Taranjit.

Yes he was a rich man now, reflected Jellicoe. He'd given no thought to what he would inherit when Sylvia died. He'd never thought to ask for the will, especially when the two investigations had been running. It wouldn't look good, Taranjit had said. No kidding.

He wondered why he'd given no thought to the money. More than this, he'd forgotten about it. Even in the worst days over the last six months as he opened up, yet another can of Heinz Baked Beans which had comprised his diet for such a long time. Monk, the cat, ate better than he did.

Monk.

He had to get back soon. The poor cat would be missing him even if he gave the impression that he could take or leave Jellicoe. Cats were good at lying. Not like dogs. You could see how they felt in their eyes, in their voices, in the wag of their tails. Not cats. Better poker players too, probably.

Taranjit was holding a cigar out for him to take. Jellicoe shook his head but managed a half smile.

'I want to live long enough to enjoy the money.'

'Let's go for a drink, Nick. Some champagne?'

'Do you mind if we don't. Seems strange,' said Jellicoe.

Taranjit clapped Jellicoe on the back gently.

'You're right. I'm sorry. Perhaps it's still too soon.'

They went, instead, for a celebratory pot of tea at a Lyons Tea Room and then parted company with a promise from Jellicoe that he would think about Taranjit's recommendations on how he would invest the money.

Jellicoe walked along the Strand unsure of where to go. He did not want to return to the hotel in Sussex Gardens he'd taken to avoid press camping out at his family home, but nor did he want to be out with people. He thought once more about the note that Claudia had sent him. Would it be in bad taste to go and see her after all that had happened, after seeing their lawyer and hearing about his inheritance from her daughter?

Perhaps she was going to demand the money back.

*

The next morning, Jellicoe took a taxi to Regent's Park. He asked the driver to park a hundred yards away from the apartment, out of sight. If Claudia was waiting for him at the window, the last thing he wanted was for her to see him stepping out of a black cab. That would be too much. They had never been close, but she didn't deserve that.

There were no clouds in the sky. It felt like a metaphor for his life, yet he could feel nothing but sorrow for the woman he was about to meet. First her daughter and now her husband. Both had died violently; unexpectedly. He wondered how she would be both with him but also within herself. She had always been difficult to read, and Jellicoe almost prided himself on his ability to understand people.

Stephen Temple had been more overt. He was a snob and had wanted better for his daughter. He suspected Claudia too, but she hid it better behind a studied indifference, a coldness that was more Aryan than Italian. Then again, she was originally from Milan. The Italians considered them German. He remembered a film that Sylvia had taken him to in Italy starring an Italian comedy actor, Toto, who was from the south. He'd gone to Milan dressed in a long fur coat and couldn't believe that it could be hot there. Even with Jellicoe's limited grasp of Italian, he'd found the scene funny and true.

Jellicoe arrived at the apartments. He didn't look up but even if he had, he knew she would stay back far enough for him not to see her, and she was there.

Claudia watched Jellicoe walk towards the apartment. She stood beside the table where just a week ago, her husband had taken his own life. She felt sorry about her husband but was not devastated by his loss. She'd lost everything she'd ever wanted a year before; the loss of her husband was no more than the distant echo of a scream.

On the desk by the window was the morning paper. It was open at a page which had a several photographs taken after the inquest. There was one of Jellicoe flanked by his mother and father and an Asian man who had acted for him. The one of Claudia was a little blurred and she was wearing sunglasses anyway. Just behind Claudia was the young woman whose testimony had effectively saved Jellicoe. She was trying to shield her face from the unrelenting, intrusive gaze of the press photographers.

Two minutes later she heard the buzzer on the door. It sounded like two angry bees arguing over territory. Stubbing out her cigarette she glided towards the front door like the ballerina she had once wanted to be. She opened the door.

Jellicoe and Claudia studied one another for a moment and then she kissed him on both cheeks. Oddly, for the first time since she'd found her husband's body, she felt a wave of unexpected emotion. Tears welled up in her eyes, and she was relieved that they did. It made it seem as if she was in mourning. Jellicoe hugged her. What else can a man do? God forbid they should speak. Who knows what nonsense would issue forth?

'Come in,' said Claudia.

Jellicoe followed her and she led him to the living room. On the table was a tray with a pot and two cups. Coffee, probably. Claudia had never taken to her adopted country's preference for tea. She gestured to the seat and sat down opposite him.

'Com'e stai Nick?' she asked. She lifted the coffee pot and poured the black liquid into the bone China tea cup.

Jellicoe watched her pour the coffee then replied, 'I'm fine, I suppose.' He started to say something about how sorry he was, but Claudia held her hand up and stopped him.

'He died a year ago Nick. I suppose we both did. She was our life, but we didn't understand this until we lost her. Then...then it was too late.'

'I am sorry, Claudia. I can't imagine...'

'You can, Nick. You know what this is like. It's not so different.'

Jellicoe looked in her eyes. They were a little red, her voice was steady. As ever, she was in control. The only time he had seen her really lose her composure was at Sylvia's funeral. This was different.

'We never really spoke after...' said Claudia and then she stopped herself. For few moments, the studied calmness seemed in danger of evaporating then she regained self-control. 'We weren't sure, Nick. It's not that we didn't believe you. Perhaps we just wanted someone to blame. I see now that was wrong. You lost someone too and we never appreciated this.'

Jellicoe was unsure what to say. Yes he had lost his wife but, oddly, like Claudia, that had also happened long before. There seemed no reason to say this, so he just nodded. They were silent for a moment while Claudia lit another cigarette. She offered Jellicoe one, but he declined. This brought a smile to her lips which emphasised her beauty as well as her age.

'You are too good Nick,' said Claudia. 'You were always too good. That was your problem with Sylvia. She wanted something more.'

'For me to be bad?' asked Jellicoe, in surprise.

'No, just to be wrong once. It's difficult to live with someone who is always in the right. It makes you want to justify their low opinion.'

'I never thought badly of Sylvia.'

Claudia smiled and nodded her thanks at the lie they both knew he was telling.

'Look, the past is gone now and besides, it's just too painful for me to deal with. I asked you here because there were some things I wanted to discuss.'

They were silent for a moment. Jellicoe glanced at the newspaper. He'd read the article earlier. He thought the photograph of him looked hideous. His face was drawn tight, his lips a thin line of tension. With his parents either side of him it looked like he was being supported down the steps. Probably he had been. Claudia's picture did her no favours either. Then, for the first time, Jellicoe noticed something he pulled the newspaper forward and looked more intently.

'What is it?' asked Claudia.

'The young woman behind you,' replied Jellicoe.

'Yes, doesn't seem very keen on being seen.'

Jellicoe nodded but said nothing to this. He'd heard in her testimony that she had been escaping a traumatic domestic situation. This had stopped her coming forward earlier. She wouldn't be happy at this photograph appearing in a national newspaper. Jellicoe sat back and studied his mother-in-law. Claudia returned his gaze.

Here it comes, thought Jellicoe. The money. Sylvia had left him over twenty thousand pounds in her will. How long would it have taken him to earn this as a policeman? Fifteen years? Perhaps more.

'It's not the money if that's what you're thinking,' said Claudia which made Jellicoe colour slightly at being so transparent. 'When I said you were always right I meant it. I think you are a good person Nick. I always suspected it, and I knew it to be so last week when the verdict came. I was actually happy for an hour and then I...'

Claudia stopped at this point to collect herself. Then she continued, 'I found out what had happened to Stephen. He blamed himself you see. I suppose he always did even during those times when we hoped it really was you, but we both knew, deep down, that you were innocent. When that young woman came forward and said that she'd seen the other man enter the cab well we knew it was not over. The investigation would have to start over, and then the truth would start to come out.'

Jellicoe looked up sharply at Claudia. The truth?

'What do you mean the truth?' asked Jellicoe. His voice was harder than he'd intended, and he instantly regretted his tone. Claudia seemed not to notice. She turned her attention to the window. There were tears rolling down her cheeks now. 'Claudia, what do you mean?'

'I have something for you, Nick,' said Claudia, avoiding a direct answer. She stood up and walked over to a sideboard. She lifted something from it and came back over to Jellicoe. She placed a photograph in front of him.

Jellicoe gazed down at his wife sitting with some men, including Stephen Temple. The man beside Sylvia had his arm around her. This wasn't the arm of someone who wished to comfort her as a friend. The smile on her face and the look that she was giving him made that all too clear. On the hand holding the champagne glass, Jellicoe could see the wedding ring he'd given her.

'I'm sorry Nick,' said Claudia, once more seeming to read his mind.

'Who are they?' asked Jellicoe, unable to hide the strain in his voice.

'I don't know,' replied Claudia. She seemed to shiver yet the room was warm. 'They are not good people Nick. Not good people at all.'

'I don't understand, Claudia. What are you telling me?' responded Jellicoe. He turned the photograph over and saw a name and a date. It looked like it had been made by the photographer. He glanced back at Claudia. She was fighting to retain control of her emotions.

'They killed her. They killed my little girl.'

Jellicoe stared at Claudia in shock. She returned the intensity of his gaze. There was hatred in her tear-stained eyes.

'Find them, Nick,' she snarled. 'Kill them. Kill them for me or so help me, I will do it myself.'

4

Somewhere near the seaside, 18th Aug 1959

Life wasn't all beer and skittles. Reg Burnett, of all people knew that. Chief Inspector Reginald Arthur Burnett. He'd seen enough misery and death to last a lifetime yet here he was still standing as happy as any married man of three score years had a right to be. Whatever her faults, and there were many, he and Mrs Burnett had made a good team. The two boys would testify to that. As a policeman of longstanding he hoped they would never have to testify to anything else. He and Mrs Burnett had stood together through the slings and whatnot of life. She was no Rita Hayworth but, then again, he was no Gary Cooper.

All of these thoughts pinballed around his head like the damn thing nearby as he waited for his two bags of chips at the Fish and Chip shop. One of the more serendipitous aspects of Reg Burnett's life was the proximity of both a chip shop and a pub to his house.

The smell of the deep fat frying the chips was like the elixir of life. Bass notes of salt and top notes of vinegar made the entire experience of waiting for chips almost intoxicating, at least it would have been had the new owner of the chip shop not decided to add a bloody pinball machine in order to extract yet more money from his credulous customers. Once upon a time Burnett could sit here and enjoy the peaceful noise of chips sizzling in the fryers. Now it was all bells and whistles and slaps on the side of the machine. The experience was different. Even the chips were more expensive now but, damn, they tasted good.

It had been in a funny sort of evening. Elsie had been in an unusually good mood. Sometimes such an atmosphere could lead to a little romance in the Burnett household. However, as she'd suggested he should pop into The Hen and Chicken for a swift half, which in practice meant a couple of pints in any man's language, this was perhaps not on the cards. As it turned out, Burnett had run into his fellow policeman, Constable Leonard Clarke. Clarke was a man of similar vintage, profession and outlook on life. They'd been friends for over two decades. The swift half had turned into a convivial four before Burnett with a roll of the eyes remembered that he'd been sent out to bring the chips home. Elsie wouldn't mind. She knew what he was like. They were a good team.

Burnett stood at the counter and stared hungrily at the chips being taken out of the fryer tank. The boy tapped the stainless-steel basket to rid the chips of the excess oil. Burnett winced at this. He'd have preferred him to retain every last delicious drop of chip fat. The newly cooked chips were placed on the heated scuttle and mixed with the last batch. Moments later the chips were scooped up and placed onto an old newspaper.

'Salt and vinegar?' asked the boy from behind the counter.

'Plenty,' replied Burnett.

A liberal sprinkling of salt was followed by a veritable dousing of vinegar on the chips. Burnett's mouth was not so much watering as experiencing a flood. By now he was almost swooning in anticipation like a schoolgirl at an Elvis concert.

The boy wrapped the chips up in several layers of sports pages. Burnett saw half a headline that Cowdrey was replacing May as captain in the test series. Burnett thanked him and took the two packets of chips from the counter. The race was on. He did not like to eat loop warm chips. They had to be hot like the tea he would have with them.

The chip shop was only one hundred yards from the Burnett household. He jogged the whole way home, a little unsteadily it must be said. All of the lights were on in the house which irritated him. Typical. He spent his life switching off lights left on by Elsie. She didn't have to pay the bills.

Burnett fairly burst through the door and plunged forward into the kitchen. The light was on there too, he thought with a flash of irritation. This was replaced slowly as he realised the house seemed empty.

In fact, all in all, Burnett was struck by the sheer silence in the house. This was not normally a silent household. There was no radio on in the kitchen; there was no sound coming from the living room where the television should have been on; there was no sound of thumping around upstairs. Elsie was a largish woman; her movements could make the house shake sometimes.

'Elsie, chips are here, dear,' shouted Burnett. Despite the unfair reputation men have for being unable to manage more than one task at a time in comparison to their more versatile other halves, Burnett shouted this while putting the kettle on before pirouetting to set out a plate for Elsie and a knife and fork. He usually ate with his fingers direct from the newspaper.

There was no reply.

'Elsie,' shouted Burnett. There was now more than a trace of irritation in his voice.

It was then he spotted an envelope lying on the table. It had his name written on it in Elsie's hand. He frowned for a moment then sat down. He picked up the envelope and tore it open. Inside was a letter. Unfolding it clumsily, he started to read. When he'd finished he set it down on the table gingerly.

'Oh Elsie,' was all he could bring himself to say. 'How could you?'

Monk the cat was sitting outside the door to Jellicoe's flat lapping the milk that his neighbour had put out for him. He glanced up sourly at Jellicoe with a 'where-have-you-been?' look that cats reserve for their subjects, never owners. Jellicoe immediately recognised the expression on the cat's face and felt duty-bound to apologise.

'Sorry old boy.'

This was never going to cut it with the black cat who turned away from him. Jellicoe opened the door and watched as Monk entered into the flat. He hadn't been inside since the previous week. The cat looked around then pottered into the kitchen, followed by Jellicoe. The detective extracted a tin of Whiskas from his pocket.

'Look what I have,' said Jellicoe hoping that this peace offering might repair their relationship.

The cat ignored him but was there just a softening in the rather cold attitude. Monk stood on the kitchen floor waiting. Jellicoe opened the drawer. This was a signal that the tin opener would soon appear. A well-choreographed routine was triggered by this action. Monk finally acknowledged the presence of Jellicoe with a miaow and then leapt with astonishing agility cat's possess onto the kitchen table which Jellicoe had long since given up stopping him from doing. He waited while Jellicoe, who still hadn't taken his coat off, dispensed the food into his bowl. Finally, the bowl was placed on the table and some form of détente was established through the agency of Whiskas cat meat.

Cat fed and watered, Jellicoe was able, at last, to take off his coat and put the kettle on. He looked around his small apartment. It felt good to be home, yet a lingering sense of dissatisfaction remained. A few days ago the case against him had been dropped and he'd found out that he was a rich man. Either event should have been a cause for celebration. Now it felt better seeing his adopted cat again; his new status seemed to matter less. His life would be easier for sure. He could quit the police force if he wanted, travel anywhere in the world.

He looked at Monk greedily wolfing down his lunch and stroked the back of the cat's head before turning to make himself some tea. Out of curiosity, he opened the cupboard and saw half a dozen tins of Heinz Beans. He smiled at the memory of his diet over the last six months or so. This would change, but would he leave the town? His job? This remained to be seen. He still hadn't received the inheritance or life assurance yet. This might take a few weeks according to Taranjit. In an unusual, perhaps, unprecedented reversal in the lawyer-client relationship, Taranjit had advanced him one thousand pounds which, by now, would be nestling comfortably in his bank account. Jellicoe had joked that Taranjit would be disbarred if anyone ever heard about this act of generosity. The lawyer pointed a finger at him and warned Jellicoe not to tell a soul.

At least his immediate money worries would be over. He glanced at the clock. It was just after ten in the morning. He would report into the station. It had been a few weeks now and

40

they might need him although the last time he spoke with Burnett his chief had said things were quiet. The criminals had gone to Spain, if they were successful, or Margate if not. The cackle that had accompanied this observation perhaps undermined its veracity somewhat.

Although he hadn't seen Burnett since leaving for London, they had stayed in contact every few days. It may have been quiet, but the usual range of misdemeanours remained in place: burglaries, shop lifting, domestic abuse, missing persons who invariably had run away from a husband or a father who had no right to be described so. Despite the range of issues they had to deal with, there were enough people around to handle them. There needed to be because Jellicoe knew that he would be getting more time off. The chief inspector would have given in to this reluctantly. He knew Burnett liked him. More than this, the chief inspector rated him. Another week would not make a difference and it would give him time to do as Claudia had requested.

This was the least he could do. She was raising no objection to him inheriting a lot of money that could just as easily have gone to her. He doubted she would miss the money much. She was rich and had married a rich man. It was the way of things, he supposed. Wealth attracts wealth. He smiled at this. Wealth attracts, end of story. He'd seen enough May to September romances to realise that much could be overlooked if the bank balance were large enough.

Jellicoe spent an hour back at his flat before making his way in to the police station. As ever, at the desk, was Sergeant 'Crumbs' Crombie. Like his friend, Constable Clarke, Crombie had served during the War. Unlike his friend, he'd come back with a lifetime reminder of what can happen when

41

bullets and bombs hit their target. Crombie had lost a leg. Despite this, the police had taken him back and assigned him a desk role. This did not stop him from, once in a while, venturing out of the station into the field.

'Nick,' greeted Crombie when he saw Jellicoe step through the doors of the station. 'It's good to have you back. We were all delighted to hear the news.'

It took a moment for it to register with Jellicoe that he was referring to the verdict from the inquest rather than his recent salvation from financial worry. He smiled back at Crombie, 'I think a celebration might be in order. Drinks will be on me.'

'Don't tell Clarkey or Reg that. They'll bankrupt you.'

As impressive as the two men were at holding their drink, it would take one almighty session for any dent to be made on his new found wealth. Still, if anyone could make a sporting go of it, he suspected the constable, and the chief inspector would be just such men.

'Maybe the first round or two then,' laughed Jellicoe as he slipped through the double doors and into the stairwell that led up to the floor where the detectives' office was located.

The men in the office greeted Jellicoe like a prodigal son returned. Wallace then Yates came over and shook his hand firmly. Further indication of their delight was the curt nod of the head and the genuine warmth of their smiles. Nothing was more was offered; nothing more was asked. This was the way of things and Jellicoe would not have it any other way. He disliked overt displays of emotion in men. It seemed unmanly. His emotions resided deep within him where none could see. He respected stoicism. Then they returned to their desks and waited for Burnett to appear from his office. There would be no more mention of the inquest. The matter was closed.

Except that it wasn't over. The killer remained at large, and Claudia wanted Jellicoe to find him.

'How are you feeling David?' asked Jellicoe as Wallace returned to his seat.

'Much better,' said Wallace. The young man only a couple of months previously had lain in a coma, near death. He'd survived and then proceeded to surprise everyone by diving straight into a case undercover and being wounded, once more, in the line of duty. Yet here he was, back and still full of the uncomplaining enthusiasm that made him such a popular member of the team.

Burnett turned away from his window as he heard the men greet Jellicoe. He'd watched Jellicoe walk into the building. There was a lightness to his step that was evident even from the second floor. This was a man for whom the weight of the world had been lifted while he was feeling desolate. He watched the men, one by one, shake the hand of Jellicoe and tell him they never doubted. They hadn't doubted. Not one of them believed that the detective inspector had murdered his wife. He caught Jellicoe's eye and, with a heart heavy with turmoil, waved him to come into the office. Jellicoe went immediately towards him.

'Hi son, come in,' said Burnett. He attempted a smile before giving it up as a bad job. 'Sit down.'

'Thanks sir,' said Jellicoe taking a seat. Burnett remained standing and turned once more to the window.

'Knew you'd win son. Never in doubt.'

'I wasn't so confident,' admitted Jellicoe.

Burnett turned to him; his large body silhouetted against the grey sky. The room seemed to be dark or perhaps it was Jellicoe's imagination.

'Are you coming back to work then?' asked Burnett. His tone was light and yet heavy at the same time like an old man trying to make conversation with a young teenager.

'Yes sir but I was hoping I could have one more week off.. Superintendent Frankie suggested two weeks, but I think that's a bit much. I have something I have to do.'

Burnett frowned and looked at Jellicoe in the eye for the first time since he'd stepped inside the office.

'How do you mean?'

Direct questions invariably meet direct part truths. No sensible person will adopt a course of outright lies when partial disclosure is an option; it protects you against tripping over your own lies, or integrity for that matter.

Jellicoe was silent for a moment. This was always fatal when dealing with a policeman. Especially when dealing with a policeman as adept at exposing lies as Burnett.

'Where do you want me to start?' said Jellicoe, exhaling heavily at the same time.

'This sounds good,' replied Burnett, taking a seat. Something in his eyes, thought Jellicoe. A moment earlier the chief inspector had seemed lost. Now he'd found him again. The pilot light was back on. Jellicoe wondered what was wrong.

Jellicoe fished in his breast pocket for his wallet. He took it out and opened it. From one of the pockets he took out the photograph Claudia had given him. Burnett looked at it without comprehending it. He turned the photograph over and tried to read the name on the back.

'Carlo Meazza.'

Burnett's pronunciation suggested only a fleeting acquaintance with foreign language: the 'z' was hissed like a snake with an abnormally high dependence on medication.

44

Jellicoe corrected him.

'Car-lo Me-at-za' said Jellicoe.

This was greeted with a withering look from Burnett. He was waking up at last. Jellicoe grinned at the reaction which further intensified Burnett's frown.

'And who is Car-lo Me-at-za?' asked Burnett in a deliberately pantomime Italian accent.

'He's a photographer,' replied Jellicoe.

Burnett rolled his eyes and snarked, 'Are you taking the mick?'

Jellicoe took the photograph back as it was in very real danger of returning to him in a half a dozen pieces.

'I don't know much about him, but he'll be able to tell me who these people are with my wife and father-in-law.'

Burnett's features softened immediately.

'I'm sorry, I should have said,' responded Burnett. He seemed genuinely aggrieved at his reaction.

Jellicoe held his hand up and replied, 'Don't, sir. Stephen and I weren't close. I think he disliked me a lot. Certainly, he did at the start. It seemed to get better in the first year and even the second but then he became a little like he had been. We weren't close. I suppose by then Sylvia, and I weren't very close either.'

'Who's the bloke?' asked Burnett. Jellicoe did not have to ask the one he meant. Burnett would have recognised his wife's face from the countless front pages that she would have appeared on following her murder and then, subsequently, when the result of the inquest was made public.

'The one with Sylvia? I have no idea. I'd certainly like to find out. Which is why I'm here.'

Eyes narrowing with suspicion, Burnett replied, 'Go on.'

45

'I want to find out who killed Sylvia. The team investigating her death have wasted a year and got nowhere. Ed Ross particularly. He couldn't find a love sock in a knocking shop.'

For the first time in that day, Burnett cracked a smile.

'Frankie would sort him out,' said Burnett. 'You know that you won't be allowed. You can have your week off, but no one will sanction you running around Italy asking questions.'

The smile left Jellicoe's face. He leaned forward.

'I don't care. If I have to go to Rome and pull the fingernails out of Rudolph Valentino here,' said Jellicoe stabbing the photograph, 'then I will.'

Burnett leaned back in his chair and smiled.

'I'm sure there's folk would pay good money to see that.' Then a thought occurred to him, and he leaned forward so that he his face was very close to Jellicoe's. 'Be careful son. There may be more to this than you think. You'll have no jurisdiction in Italy. Can you even speak the language?'

'Yes,' said Jellicoe. This was not quite true; he had a very good grasp but was far from fluent. Still, it impressed Burnett. The chief inspector rolled his eyes.

'You would,' replied Burnett sourly. He shook his head and exhaled slowly. There was probably little he could do never mind say to stop the young detective going. Quite how he would finance the trip was beyond him and how he could expect to make any progress without having any contacts in Rome, without having the case file. Basically he had nothing. Burnett told him all this. Jellicoe listened in silence, nodding only occasionally.

Finally, Jellicoe spoke up.

'I may have more of a chance than you think.'

Burnett eyed him closely, 'Oh aye?'

Jellicoe told him about the conversation with Claudia, omitting only her desire that the killer meet with a violent end. The emptiness seemed to return to Burnett's eyes as Jellicoe spoke. For a moment he wondered if he was boring his chief inspector. He thought about saying as much but something held him back.

'You've booked a flight to Rome then?'

'Yes,' said Jellicoe. 'I fly tomorrow morning at ten.'

'So much for asking permission,' observed Burnett.

Jellicoe grinned and shrugged. Then he said, 'I knew you'd be sympathetic.'

Burnett's level of sympathy extended to telling Jellicoe that he would leave the office at the toe end of his boot. Jellicoe took this to mean that permission for his extended leave had been granted.

'Do I need to go to the Superintendent?' asked Jellicoe on the way out. 'He knows about the week off but not what I intend doing.'

'Leave him to me,' replied Burnett wearily. He turned, once more, and began staring out of the window.

What was up with him wondered Jellicoe? The outer office had emptied with only Wallace left. Jellicoe walked over to Wallace. He could see that the hair had grown back now over where they had shaved his head to operate.

'Are you sure you're ready?' asked Jellicoe. Wallace grinned but made no reply. Certainly, the colour was back on his cheeks, and he'd regained a lot of the weight he'd lost. 'Is everything all right with the chief inspector. He seems a bit...' Jellicoe paused unsure of how to describe him. 'He doesn't seem himself.'

Wallace shrugged.

'He was with Widow Twanky earlier,' said Wallace, in reference to Superintendent Frankie. 'Maybe that's put him in a bad mood.'

Jellicoe shook his head and replied, 'He's not in a bad mood. He just seems a bit low. Anyway, David, I'm not going to be around for a week.'

Wallace glanced up in surprise.

'More holiday?' grinned the young detective sergeant. In any other policeman especially a subordinate, this might have been deemed insubordination. With Wallace, who was well-liked by all, it was just part of his natural effervesce which nobody minded.

'I wish,' replied Jellicoe. 'I'll see you in a week or so. Try not to get into trouble.'

'Don't you get into any more trouble either, sir,' replied Wallace, still smiling.

*

Jellicoe had one more stop to make before he returned to London that evening. It was to a small bungalow near the outskirts of the town. The front of the house was a riot of colour: roses, rhododendrons and other flowers that he probably should know. However, like most young men, he had not yet developed sufficient interest in flowers beyond their almost magical powers in casting a spell over the opposite sex.

He knocked on the door. A dog began to bark, and then another. One was deep and loud, the other more from the yapping end of the spectrum. The door opened and an elderly lady greeted Jellicoe.

'Detective Inspector Jellicoe, will you come inside for a tea?'

'No thanks, Mrs Bickerstaff.'

Ada Bickerstaff had, on occasion, provided help to the police. She was a widow of a certain age; an age around seventy but she admitted to sixty.

Jellicoe held out a set of keys.

'Monk is usually waiting around six in the evening. I've left enough cat food to last a couple of weeks. If you could make a fuss of him I would appreciate it. I suspect my neighbour just rushes in and out to feed him. He's quite friendly. Well, as friendly as any cat I suppose.'

There was more barking from inside the house. Ada Bickerstaff rolled her eyes and took the keys from Jellicoe.

'Don't worry, I'll look after him, lad, and, by the way, I was delighted when I heard the verdict. I never doubted you.'

Jellicoe smiled but could not say anything. He was oddly moved by the unquestioning confidence from the woman before him. They parted on this note and Jellicoe turned to walk up the short driveway. A busy week lay ahead. Wallace's words echoed in his head: don't get into trouble either.

Never were words more thoroughly ignored.

6

'Do you have everything, son?' asked James Jellicoe of his son. They were parked outside the Europa Building at Heathrow airport. Jellicoe nodded his head but patted his breast pocket anyway to check his passport was there. He reached over to the back seat of the Wolseley and lifted a thick Manila file. He glanced once more at his father.

'If you lose that, don't even think about coming back son,' said the Jellicoe the elder. 'I'll have your guts for garters.'

'You'll be in prison by then,' pointed out Jellicoe to his father. The tone was light, but the message was all too clear. Written on the outside of the Manila file were three words: 'Black Cab Murders'. His father as an Assistant Chief Constable at the Metropolitan Police would have access to almost all ongoing case files. That he had managed to make a copy of key aspects of the case was a minor miracle. The risk he was taking in handing them over to his son went, as Jellicoe suggested, beyond his immediate career prospects.

Jellicoe stepped outside the car and went to the boot to take his suitcase. He saw a policeman approach their car to warn them to leave. Then the policeman saw James Jellicoe's uniform and then the insignia. He gave a salute and walked on.

Jellicoe's father stepped out of the car. The two men regarded one another.

'This is madness, Nick.'

Jellicoe erupted into laughter and replied, 'Thanks for the support, dad.' He was genuinely amused and actually quite pleased. His father had never been one to shy away from difficult conversations. He was straight and Jellicoe appreciated his honesty. Then James Jellicoe smiled at his son.

'If anyone can do this, son, it's you but I'm just being honest. You're on your own. You're in a foreign city. You know no one, well not many anyway. I don't even know how I would begin to investigate but then again I'm not like you or your grandad.'

'I'll bring him back a souvenir,' replied Jellicoe as he thought of his elderly grandfather, a man who had been part of a long line of the Jellicoe family who had served in the police force.

'Find the man who killed Sylvia and come home safely. That's all he or any of us want,' said Jellicoe's father who had to raise his voice to make himself heard over the sound of an aeroplane taking off.

It was time to go. There was nothing more to be said and Englishmen were not brought up to say it. Jellicoe nodded to his father and the two men shook hands. Then Jellicoe headed through the doors of the terminal without looking back at a man who was not looking at him.

The terminal was crowded with men wearing dark suits. There were not many women and those that Jellicoe could see were wearing hostess uniforms. Jellicoe headed towards the board to see where he needed to check in. The flight to Rome was an hour away. Thankfully, there were no delays. He was heading in the direction of the check in when he heard a voice shouting behind him.

'Nick wait up, son. It's me.'

Nick spun around to locate the source of the shouting. His jaw almost dropped when he saw who it was.

Dressed in his usual crumpled wool suit running towards him clutching a brown leather suitcase was Chief Inspector Reginald Burnett. He waved at Jellicoe when he saw him looking over with a quizzical expression.

Burnett stopped running and ambled over. He was not really designed for extreme exertion being a few pounds heavier than his five-foot eight height ideally should sustain.

'Thank God for that,' said Burnett. 'I thought I had the wrong flight.'

'Flight?' exclaimed Jellicoe. 'What flight?'

'Rome, son. You didn't think I was going to let you do this on your own did you?' Burnett glanced down at the Manila file underneath Jellicoe's arm. 'Oh aye, son? Is that a bit of bedtime reading from your father?'

Jellicoe glanced down at the case file and coloured slightly. Then he frowned.

'Have you taken time off?'

'Yes, you don't think I called in sick do you? Widow Twankie approved it. I put Davies in charge. He gave me a week's compassionate leave.'

This took Jellicoe aback. His brow furrowed.

'Is everything all right, sir?' asked Jellicoe. He remembered how Burnett had seemed at a low ebb the day before.

'Been better son,' admitted Burnett. Just then the two men heard over the tannoy a boarding call for passengers to Rome. 'I'll tell you on the plane. Let's get a move on.'

Fifteen minutes later they were walking across the tarmac towards the BOAC de Havilland Comet.

'Not sure I trust these bloody things,' said Burnett, looking sourly at the aircraft. It was a matter of conjecture on just what exactly Burnett did trust although Jellicoe suspected that he and Constable Clarke would be on a short list. At least where the aircraft was concerned, Burnett did have cause to be worried. The Comet had experienced a number of fatal crashes in the early fifties and even one minor one at Ciampino airport in Rome where they were bound.

'Don't worry,' said Jellicoe. 'I've been on this aeroplane a number of times. It's fine.'

The expression on Burnett's face suggested that this reassurance was likely to fall on deaf ears. They climbed the steps into the plane. Burnett's expression, which lay somewhere between unhappy and Basset hound, perked up when an attractive stewardess welcomed him on board. He smiled back before raising his eyebrow to the amused Jellicoe.

'You've changed your tune,' noted Jellicoe as they sat down.

'Best give it a chance,' replied Burnett looking around at the other passengers. They were mostly men over thirty dressed in dark suits.

'So, you were going to tell me about what brings you here,' prompted Jellicoe to Burnett who was happily taking in the view of another stewardess who had passed them in the slim aircraft corridor.

'I wonder who hires them?' mused Burnett.

'Fancy a career change?'

Burnett grinned his answer. Then his face became more serious. Jellicoe braced himself for the answer to his question.

'Elsie's left me.'

Jellicoe had never met Elsie but had it on good authority that Burnett's status as chief ended at the front door of their house. From that point only one person ruled the roost. Clarkey had described her as one part Tessie O'Shea, one part Stalag Commandant. She did have her bad points too, apparently. Still, it was clear that the chief was in shock, although the current grin on his face might just be a sign that he was slowly coming to terms with the pain.

'What happened?'

Burnett inhaled slowly and looked at Jellicoe.

'I'm not saying everything was perfect between us, but we had over thirty years together. Two lads n'all. Two nights ago, I went out to the chippy. She said she didn't feel like cooking, which was a relief. She wanted some chips. Usually that means she's happy for me to have a swift one. As it happens, I met up with Clarkey, so we had a couple then I went to get the chips. When I got back to the house she was gone. She left a letter.'

'What did it say?' asked Jellicoe, himself no stranger to what happens as a marriage slowly disintegrates.

'She'd run off with Derek the milkman,' said Burnett with something close to his old snarl. 'Total waste of money that second bag of chips.'

Jellicoe nodded, 'Yes, I can see that.'

'That Derek Titmus is always at it. I reckon a few of the kids round our way are his. There's a few ginger kids.'

'He has ginger hair then?'

'Do you know him?'

'Just a guess,' replied Jellicoe. 'Are you going to try and get her back?'

'Am I hell. She's made her bed and she's probably lying in it right now,' answered Burnett angrily. There was a tinge of sadness in his voice too as it occurred to him what might be happening at that very moment in the imaginary bed. He grimaced slightly.

'Something wrong?' asked Jellicoe.

'No, she's a big lass, is Elsie. Titmus is a bit of a weed. She'll flatten him.'

'Serve him right,' suggested Jellicoe. 'I'm sorry chief.'

'What for?' asked Burnett.

'The chips. What do you bloody think?'

For the first time since he'd seen Burnett since the inquest, he managed to raise a chuckle. The two men ended the conversation as the stewardess took them through a pre-flight safety briefing. Soon they were taking off. Burnett gripped the arms of the seat tightly as the plane tilted upwards.

'How long is this bloody flight?' he asked irritably.

7

South London: 20th August 1959

Joseph Sanders was just over six feet tall, well made with a thin moustache that, along with his slicked back hair, made him look like a spiv. He always liked to dress well; suits looked good on his tall, slender frame. Aside from his attire he had a manner that could be charming when required. Once upon a time he'd thought about becoming a copper. Then he'd heard how much they earned. Another career suggested itself which put him on the other side of the fence from the law.

Although well-made he was not a brave man. Nor was he likely to threaten Bertrand Russell in the intelligence stakes. The prospect of planning and executing a bank raid or a jewellery shop was as unenticing as it was unworkable. He knew his limits. The risks associated with these crimes far outweighed the, admittedly, high rewards. Instead, he travelled around confining his unlawful activities to low key smash and grabs. Televisions, radios, toasters were his speciality. A brick through a window to any shop naïve enough to leave such goods in the window. Asking for it they were.

Of course, after ten years he was always likely to have a few run ins with the law. So far they had never managed to catch him in the act, and he had enough friends who would confirm that he had been in a card game when any crime was taking place. In fact, the police had long suspected this was nonsense, but they lacked the manpower to keep an eye on him long enough to catch him in the act. Or perhaps, the very limits of his ambition inoculated him against the police spending too much of their valuable time on him.

Another safeguard was his willingness to travel around the city to do his job. He developed a series of contacts that he could fence what he acquired within an hour. Nothing stayed long in his hands.

Sanders neither loved his life nor sought to improve it. He lived one day at a time, always having enough on his pocket to spend on the things he liked: clothes, cigarettes and a good whisky.

Then he met Susan.

Suze.

She was an assistant at a department store where he'd gone to buy a new suit following one particularly lucrative evening's work in Clapham. Her dark eyes had captured his attention as well as her youth and guilelessness. There was something about her that seemed untouched, and he was just the man to find out if his instinct was correct. His pursuit of her began that day. He bought a suit that was a little bit more expensive than he'd intended. He saw it as an investment.

Suze was impressed and delighted. He'd made it seem like she had persuaded him. For one awful moment he had tried on an even more expensive Italian suit, but she preferred the one he eventually bought. This was just as well as he certainly couldn't have afforded the other.

The suggestion of a date seemed as natural as asking about the weather. She was hesitant at first, but Sanders was too long in the game not to know how to reel her in. He'd smiled and thanked her for her help and turned to go away. She'd called out to him.

Always works, he thought.

He took things slowly. The first kiss was on the second date. This had surprised her. He hadn't stinted on dinner.

Always works.

Two weeks later his instincts about Suze had proven correct. She took to her new life with something close to abandon. Twenty-one years old, still living at home with parents who attended church. If only they knew, he thought.

And then they did. There was no hiding it in fact. He'd wanted to take her to someone he knew. She wouldn't hear of it. A week later she had been thrown out of the house by her father. There was nowhere else to go but to Sanders' small flat.

It's different when they're with you all the time his friends had warned him. Boy was this true. Now she knew the truth about him too. She knew what he was, what he did every evening but there was a baby to think of, so she accepted it. She even accepted it the first time he'd slapped her. Afterwards he was apologetic but still, something had changed. It was the look on his face that hurt almost as much as the stinging on her cheek. Almost.

Things went downhill from there. He had no idea how to deal with a young woman outside of the bedroom never mind one who was pregnant. It was easier to go out on jobs. This did not make her happy. She did not like the risks he took, she did not like the way of life, she didn't like being left alone at night with her thoughts and worries and growing doubts. If you don't like it you know where the bloody door is he would say. That shut her up.

As she grew in size the less she attracted him. The beauty that he'd once known seemed to have disappeared. Soon he realised she revolted him. Insofar as there had ever been any love it was now extinguished. His irritation grew by the day: her weakness, her neediness. The tears. Bloody hell, the constant crying over something or other. The only way to get that under control was a slap. Not too hard mind. Just something to bring her to her senses.

It usually worked. She would disappear off to the bedroom. At least if she were sobbing he couldn't see it, hear it. There'd be enough of that when the baby came. Maybe it would take her mind off him.

Once you start, though. The first slap he'd felt bad about. Slowly it became the way he kept control of the house and order in his life. The mute rebellion was there but where could she go? That was both a problem for her and for him. The parents' wouldn't speak to her now unless she got married, and there was no way he was going to do that.

He was doing a job when Billy arrived. To be fair, he'd grown more attached to the little lad than he'd ever imagined he would. The way they look at you. The smile. For the first time in his life he felt a degree of responsibility. Suze had even spruced herself up a bit. Things were better.

He even tried looking for a job. Alas any interview only lasted as long as it came to explaining his long without work or lack of references. He had some faked by a friend but when he started the job it was clear he did not know what he was doing.

That's when the arguments started again. She wanted a ring, he wanted to wring her neck, and the baby wouldn't stop crying. He spent as much time away from the flat as he could.

What did he know about bringing up children? The kid needed grandparents. They tried again.

The grandparents weren't interested, and they said she said he was an awful man. He had nothing on her parents. Now they were truly hypocrites. At least he made no apology for what he was.

The morning she left seemed like all of the others. He'd come home from his latest straight job, a bar if memory served, and fall into bed. The night would be disrupted as usual by Billy crying. The next morning he and Suze would both be a bit irritable. He'd never have touched the baby. He only wanted to show Suze how it was done. Not that he knew. He wanted her to be a bit more proactive, but she'd misunderstood. Bloody women.

She'd been gone a year now. No sign of her. He didn't start looking until a week later. She really was gone. No one had seen her. A part of him was relieved. Another part felt a burning humiliation. His friends would mock him. She's run off with her fancy man has she? The real dad. That was the one that got him. The real dad. He'd have her life if that was the case. No one, and I mean no one, did that to Joe Sanders without living to regret it.

He put the word out. Anyone who sees Suze and the baby was to let him know. He had a bit of money now. Bar work didn't pay but it introduced him to a new boss. This was a man who paid well, who looked after his men. You could make a lot of money dealing drugs, and it was safe too. He sold mainly to middle class professionals in the city. Lord, if the banks only knew what their younger staff members were doing they'd have a stroke.

Yes, he had a bit of money now, and he wanted his boy back.

His son.

He looked at the newspaper photograph. It was her all right. Tried to shield herself from the photographer. Fancy that. His Suze the key witness at an inquest, and the famous Black Cab Killer too. Who'd have thought.

Sanders turned to his friend, Barry Cooper. Everyone called him 'Gary' principally because he looked nothing like the American actor. Cooper was even taller than Sanders and built like a light heavyweight. He'd tried the ring but a combination of a glass jaw and having a neck like a llama convinced him that there were easier ways to make money than being used as a punch bag by aspiring young fighters.

'See anyone you know there Gary?'

Cooper studied the photographs in the paper.

'I recognise the copper. He didn't kill his bird then?'

'Apparently not. That's not the picture I meant. Look at the other one.'

Cooper studied the picture for a few moments.

'Looks like that Italian bird, Gina whatsit.'

Sanders looked at the picture again and smile, 'Gina Lollobrigida. You're right Gary. Not bad for an old bird. Not her; look behind.'

He thrust the paper into Cooper's hands. The Londoner studied the picture once more. Then a slow smile spread over his face.

'Bloody hell. Is that Suze?'

'Yes,' confirmed Sanders. 'That's Suze. We need to find her.'

'Why? I thought you were well rid of her.'

'Well, maybe I was, maybe I wasn't. She has my little lad. Easty likes his boys to be family men. He wants us to be settled, you know, trustworthy. He's got a business to run. Who needs lots of young lads full of themselves causing trouble? Much better to have older hands, with their feet on the ground. Businessmen. I reckon it'd be a nice surprise for him if he saw me with my kid. Could mean promotion, and you know what that means?'

Cooper hadn't a clue, but he smiled anyway and nodded. This was misconstrued by Sanders.

'Exactly. More money, Gary. More money.'

Now it all made sense and even Cooper could see where this train was headed.

'We should try and find Suze,' said Cooper.

'We should try and find Suze,' confirmed Sanders.

⬜

8

Ciampino Airport, Rome: 20th August 1959

'We are coming into land,' said the captain.

There can be few words that prompt as much relief and terror among men and women as these. Burnett gripped the seat while Jellicoe looked on in amusement. This was met with a few well-chosen words from the chief that only provoked laughter from his insubordinate subordinate.

The landing took place without incident and soon they were on the tarmac walking towards the two-story terminal building.

'Not very big is it?' said Burnett looking on unimpressed.

'It's not quite Heathrow,' acknowledged Jellicoe. 'They're building a bigger one out towards the coast.'

As they strolled through the terminal building, past the people waiting for their friends and family, Jellicoe spotted a black and white cat in sitting on one of the chairs. He smiled and went over to it.

'What are you doing?' demanded Burnett.

'He's always here,' said Jellicoe.

They moved on a few moments later. When they reached the exit Burnett pointed to a sign.

'Buses to the left.'

'Let's take a taxi,' suggested Jellicoe.

Burnett stared in horror at Jellicoe.

'That'll cost an arm and a leg.'

'Wait till you see the hotel,' said Jellicoe as he started towards the taxi.

On the way in to Rome they passed a large sand coloured building built in an art deco style of the late thirties. Jellicoe pointed it out to Burnett.

'That's Cinecittà.' He pronounced it chin-ay-cheetah. 'Biggest film studio in Europe. They're making Ben Hur there. Last time I was over I bumped into Charlton Heston.'

This seemed to impress Burnett momentarily then he said, 'Did he ask you for an autograph?'

This was a reference to a running joke at the police station related to Jellicoe's passing resemblance to the English actor Anthony Steel. Jellicoe smiled at this and replied, 'Apparently Anthony Steel lives here in Rome.'

The taxi took them along Via Tuscolana one of the main old Roman roads that led to the centre of the city. By now Burnett had removed his jacket and tie. His face was redder than a lobster in a gym. Perspiration ran in rivulets down his face. Jellicoe glanced at the wool suit and said, 'We'll have to get you something decent to wear. We'll do that after we check in.'

'Where am I getting the money for a new suit?' said Burnett sourly. 'This bloody taxi is going to cost me an arm and a leg.'

'As I said, wait till you see the hotel,' repeated Jellicoe. Then he added, 'Don't worry. It's on me.'

Burnett turned and looked at him, a frown on his face.

'Go on,' he said.

'I inherited a lot of money. It had been held back until the inquest confirmed that there was no case against me.'

'I won't ask how much.'

No one asks how much which is usually a signal that they are desperate to know. Jellicoe knew this as well as Burnett. As tempting as it was to string it out a little longer, Jellicoe opted for full disclosure. He told Burnett the amount.

'How much?' exclaimed Burnett in shock.

'Twenty thousand. There's some life assurance in there too.'

Confirmation that his ears had not deceived him was greeted with the very best words that Anglo Saxon can offer upon hearing such a revelation.

Ten minutes later the taxi turned past Villa Borghese and onto Via Veneto. When Jellicoe pointed to their hotel, Burnett treated him to a few other words of congratulation or something not very like that.

The sign on the front of the hotel read: Hotel Grand Flora. Jellicoe paid the driver, and they stepped out into the cauldron of Rome. Burnett looked around him with in awe. On one side of the hotel, across the road was an ancient Roman wall built high with pale red brick. The hotel, designed in a neoclassical style, was a blinding white which made Burnett's eyes water. Jellicoe was, by now, wearing dark sunglasses.

'Different world,' said Burnett, as the two men walked past the hotel doorman into an expansive reception area.

The man on reception took one look at Burnett, who was minus jacket and tie with some of his shirt peeking out over his trousers, and immediately began to speak English. He nudged Jellicoe and tilted his head to acknowledge the Italian's perceptiveness after Jellicoe had booked a twin room.

'Smart lad that,' observed Burnett as they walked towards the elevator.

'Why? Most hotel receptionists speak a bit of English.'

'Aye, but how did he know?'

Jellicoe glanced at the dishevelled chief.

'I'm going to treat you to a new suit, chief, otherwise you're going to melt away. Then we'll start the investigation.'

'I don't see what's wrong with this,' said Burnett in an offended voice.

'Trust me. You'll feel like a new man.'

Half an hour later the two men climbed out of their taxi and stood outside a men's shop on Via Barberini. The name of the shop was Brioni. Burnett followed Jellicoe to the front door. Burnett looked at the suits in the ship window. They looked expensive. Then he saw the prices.

'You've got to be f....'

Jellicoe was already through the front door. The eyes of the shop assistant widened in surprise then narrowed to a frown. It was a reaction Jellicoe was used to in Rome. The frown of the shop assistant deepened when Burnett appeared. The assistant looked like a film star and certainly dressed like one. His suit was black with a white shirt and a thin black silk tie.

Jellicoe spoke in Italian to the assistant.

'Have you a light suit that will fit my friend? A couple of shirts and ties too while we're at it, and a dinner suit, too. For us both.'

The shop assistant was caught between shock at the extent of the challenge that had been set and greed at the thought of the bonus he would receive. He strode towards Burnett in a threatening manner. He put a hand on each of Burnett's arms and regarded him like he would a work of art, minus the appreciation and minus the art.

'What on earth did you say to him?' said Burnett in a stage whisper.

'I told him that you liked young Italian men.'

Burnett's reply was a succinct reminder that he was, technically, still his superior officer but Jellicoe was laughing too much to hear.

The following few minutes saw Burnett's level of discomfort grow along with Jellicoe's amusement. The shop assistant, whose name was Lorenzo, wielded his tape measure like a surgical knife. There was hardly a part of Burnett's body that was not measured. Twice. Thankfully, Lorenzo did not understand Burnett's smirking advice to allow extra room around his crotch.

'Around your waist you mean,' suggested Jellicoe.

The forensic examination of Burnett's figure completed; the shop assistant went away to find something from the ready-to-wear section. He came back with a powder blue suit that even Burnett looked at without his usual vinegary expression. The jacket fitted perfectly but the waist needed to be let out on the trousers.

'Can you do it now?' asked Jellicoe.

'Half an hour,' said Lorenzo.

'We'll go for a coffee,' replied Jellicoe. 'Pick out some ties and three white shirts too, please, and a couple of white shirts for me.' He added his collar size and a two minutes later they were out of the shop and walking towards a bar.

Music was playing in the bar as they entered. A female vocalist was singing on the radio, 'Tinterella La Luna' Jellicoe was not a fan of rock n' roll but he liked this.

He turned to Burnett and asked, 'What would you like?'

'I'm busting for a cuppa,' said Burnett.

Jellicoe went to pay for the drinks a returned a few minutes later with the two drinks..

'What's this?' said Burnett staring at the insipid brown liquid and the dish with two slices of lemon. Jellicoe grinned.

'Welcome to Italy.'

'Do they not know how to make a bloody tea? What's that you're having?'

Jellicoe replied, 'A cappuccino.'

'Those things are just hot milk if you ask me. Bloody hell,' said Burnett. He stood up and asked Jellicoe the word for milk. La-tay came the reply. Jellicoe sat back to watch the show. Burnett strolled up with a confident air to the man at the bar with his cup of tea. He pointed to it and in a very clear voice said, 'La-tay.' Having done this he turned to Jellicoe and gave a nod.

'La-tay,' repeated the bar man looking at the tea. He seemed confused. He shook his head before saying, 'Non. Tay.'

Burnett was not a man famed for his patience.

'I can bloody well see it's tea. I want milk. La-tay,' snarled Burnett pointing to the cup.

The barman turned to Jellicoe and shrugged. It was clear he thought he was dealing with someone who was either a madman or an idiot.

'Vuole un po di latte mettere in tè.' (He wants some milk to put in his tea)

The barman frowned and shrugged. He poured some milk into a metal jug and proceeded to heat it. Then he went over to the tea and poured it. He smiled in triumph.

Burnett was even more appalled by the hot milk invading his tea. He stalked away from the bar and sat down with a thud.

'Are these people completely uncivilised?'

'I imagine they think that of us. Don't forget the Romans brought roads, baths, aqueducts to Britain. We owe them a lot.'

'Price of that bloody suit and you'll have paid them back. Hurry up and drink your coffee.'

'Ca-fay,' replied Jellicoe.

Burnett's response also made sure to emphasize the pronunciation of each syllable although it was definitely not Latin in origin.

They returned to the Brioni shop where Lorenzo confirmed that the trousers were ready. At the changing room, Burnett handed out his suit and shirt from behind the curtain. Jellicoe handed it to Lorenzo with the instruction that it should be hung in the nearest bin. This brought a smile from the shop assistant.

Burnett finally appeared from behind the curtain in his new suit. He patted his stomach and gave a nod of approval. The suit fitted him perfectly now and represented a distinct improvement on his previous apparel which he admitted when he saw Jellicoe.

'A sack cloth would have been an improvement,' noted Jellicoe but Burnett was in much too good a mood to argue. A Panama hat was added to the bill thereby completing the look.

'Tell you what, I wish Elsie could see me now,' said Burnett as he stopped by a mirror near the exit of the shop. Then the smile left his face. Jellicoe patted him on the back.

'Let's put these shirts back in the room. Enough shopping,' said Jellicoe.

Burnett was still staring at his reflection. It was if he was looking at himself in a different language. He turned to Jellicoe and said, 'Son, this cost a packet. Are you sure?'

'I'm sure.

'I'll say this for you son, fifteen minutes to buy a new suit. If I were shopping with my Elsie it would have been an hour, and don't remind me about how she then start bartering with the shop assistant. I just wanted to hide.'

'Let's go,' replied Jellicoe.

Burnett seemed uncomfortable. Then with what appeared to be an effort of will he said, 'Thanks, Nick.'

⬚

9

Einstein is reputed to have said that the difference between genius and stupidity is that genius has its limits. Had Chief Inspector Reg Burnett known this then he would have felt pleased to be so highly esteemed because right at that moment he knew with a clear and unambiguous certainty what he was and was not capable of.

'I'm not getting on that,' said Burnett folding his arms. He looked like a five-year-old child moments away from an almighty tantrum. The cause of this particular disagreement was the object that Jellicoe was standing beside.

'It's not that bad,' said Jellicoe. 'If you're not prepared to use one yourself then you'll have to come with me.'

'Do you know what we'll look like? We'll look like a couple of p...' Burnett's assessment was lost on the sound of a Ferrari roaring past but it Jellicoe guessed he was referring to something that was still illegal in both Italy and his home country. Before Jellicoe could respond, Burnett added, 'Anyway I'll never fit.'

'Of course you will.'

'Look at the size of it,' complained Burnett but some of the power was draining from his argument.

The beige Vespa did look a little bit too small to accommodate both Jellicoe and a man who was no longer the lithe athlete of yesteryear. Jellicoe ignored the pleas of his commanding officer and handed over money to the man at the garage. He paid in advance for a week's use of the scooter before swinging his leg over the seat. Burnett made one final appeal to common sense or, at least, Jellicoe's humanity.

'It'll ruin the new suit.'

'Don't be silly. Get on.'

'Is there no helmet?'

'We're in Italy. They arrest you if you wear one.'

'Bloody hell,' responded Burnett as he reluctantly took up his pillion position. He growled, 'Don't you dare go fast.'

As much as he would have liked to, this was unlikely given Jellicoe weighed just over middleweight while Burnett would certainly have been a couple of divisions higher. The Vespa took off under Jellicoe's assured touch and joined the light traffic.

Rome in August was, as Burnett had observed, very hot but this fact was also noticed by the Roman population who left the city in droves to go to the seaside. This point was a worry for Jellicoe, but he would deal with this if it became a problem. There were not many cars on the road and those that came near the Vespa were met with a volley of abuse from Jellicoe's nervous passenger.

The two men travelled at a conservative speed through down Barberini. It was only after they had been travelling for a few minutes that Burnett, having become more reassured found himself wondering where they were going. Such a question was never going to remain unasked for long.

'Where are we going?'

'Quick tour. I want to refamiliarize myself with the city. Enjoy the view. This is the greatest and certainly the biggest museum in the world and it's a city,' replied Jellicoe.

The tour took less than twenty minutes but gave Burnett the opportunity to visit things he'd only ever seen in picture books: the Coliseum, the Forum, Trevi Fountain and Vittorio Emanuele II Monument which was Burnett's favourite until Jellicoe informed him it was not part of ancient Rome, but something built by the Fascists.

'Much as I appreciate the tour, aren't we wasting time?' asked Burnett, as the two men entered Piazza d'Espagna, home of the Spanish Steps. When Burnett saw them he smiled, 'They were in that film weren't they?'

'Yes, Audrey,' replied Jellicoe as he brought the scooter to a halt. The two men climbed off.

'So is this another part of the tour?'

'No we're meeting an old friend.'

'Who?' asked Burnett. Just then he heard a man's voice shouting.'

'Hey, Nicky boy.'

As an avid fan of American film noir and gangster movies, Burnett immediately recognised the American accent. He turned in the direction of the voice. He saw a short, rather burly looking man approach them. The man was being pulled along by a small dog.

'Culver,' said Jellicoe with a broad grin. 'Good to see you again. This is my boss, Chief Inspector Reg Burnett.' Jellicoe knelt down to stroke the dog.

'Hiya Reg, any friend of Nick is a friend of mine,' said Culver. 'This is Marilyn by the way. After Marilyn Monroe.'

'I can see the resemblance,' noted Burnett.

The Marilyn in question was a British Bulldog. She was panting heavily now having exhausted her very limited reserves on the slow trot towards Jellicoe. Burnett knelt down to stroke Marilyn and was rewarded with a tongue caressing his cheek.

'She's very affectionate,' reported Culver with pride.

Culver Wendell was an American ex-serviceman who decided to stay in Italy after the war. The first time he set foot in Italy was at Anzio. By the time he had turned twenty-one he was already a sergeant. A fondness for beer was matched only by his dislike of authority. This limited his progress within the ranks of the US Army but earned the undying love of the men in his platoon. Most of them made it through to the end of the war thanks to a combination of Culver's astonishing bravery and his willingness to turn a deaf ear to orders that he considered dumb.

Rather than return to the States he stayed in Germany first until he was demobbed and then returned to Italy, a country he had fallen in love with.

'You still on obits?' asked Jellicoe rising to his feet again.

'Of course,' replied Culver. 'Easiest damn job in the paper.'

'Obits?' asked Burnett. He too had risen to his feet again. He borrowed a handkerchief from Jellicoe to dry a face that had been positively drenched by Marilyn.

'She likes you,' observed Culver with a grin.

'Probably thinks it's her twin brother,' added Jellicoe.

Burnett ignored him and studied the little American. His hair was dark, but his skin suggested that he was not a native of the country. He wore a linen suit yet, like Burnett but not like Jellicoe, appeared to be melting in the heat.

'Obituaries,' replied Culver. 'Been doing them for ten years now. They started me on sports, but I could never take to soccer.'

'Football,' growled Burnett but there was humour in his eyes.

'Bunch of ballerinas if you ask me,' snapped back Culver, enjoying the repartee.

'You wouldn't say that on a wet Wednesday night in Stockport.'

'That you team?'

'No they're rubbish,' said Burnett with a chuckle.

They were walking towards the steps now. At the foot of the steps to the left was a tall, grey, eighteenth-century building.

'You're not,' said Culver stopping for a second. 'Last time I was there was with you.'

'It's for the chief's benefit,' replied Jellicoe.

The building in front of them was a restaurant called Babbington's. Founded by a couple of Scottish sisters, Isabel and Anna Maria Babbington in 1893, it had survived two world wars and fascism to become a Roman institution frequented by tourists as well as movie stars and politicians. As they entered the foyer of the Tea Room they passed a cat who appeared to be acting as doorman.

'Hiya Mascherino,' said Culver. Marilyn and Mascherino studiously ignored one another. Burnett gazed upwards and saw that he now had to negotiate a winding staircase. Marilyn growled also, no more enamoured by the prospect.

'Let me,' said Jellicoe picking the Bulldog up. They ascended the stairs and entered a high-ceilinged room with sunlight flooding through. Burnett liked the airiness of the room that was at once Italian yet with more than a hint of

England to civilise it. Once the orders were taken Jellicoe fished out the photograph of his father-in-law with Sylvia and the mysterious men.

'Do you know any of these men?'

'Aside from Sylvia, sorry man. I should have said before now. Isn't that her pops?' He was pointing to Stephen Temple.

Jellicoe waved this away and left Culver to gaze at the photo. Then he turned it around and read the name of the photographer.

'I've heard of this this guy, but I've never met him. Carlo Meazza is a pretty famous fashion photographer now. Does a lot of big shoots for Vogue in Italy and for the films down at Cinecittà. Have you seen the billboards with Emilia? You know the one advertising Chanel. That's one of his. When was this taken?'

'It was late fifty-seven, December according to the original photograph,' said Jellicoe. He studied Culver for a second. There was a frown on his friend's face. 'Why do you ask?'

'I guess I was surprised that this had been taken by Meazza, but if it's fifty-seven then I buy it. He used to be one of the pack of photographers that follow the stars around Via Veneto but then he caught a break when he discovered Emilia. Eighteen and stacked in the right places. He made her a big star and made himself the man every model, every film star and every magazine wanted.

'You don't know the others?'

'Sorry man, just your father-in-law and Sylvia. How is the sonovabitch?'

'He killed himself a week ago.'

Culver's eyes snapped open, and he leaned forward.

'Man, I hadn't heard. I'm sorry.'

Jellicoe nodded but could say nothing to this. There was no point in being a hypocrite about it. Yet, at the same time, he could not avoid feeling a degree of sadness for a man who could not bear to face his loss. His grief made this explicable but something in Claudia's insistence that he investigate made him wonder what else had driven him to this desperate last act.

'Where are they?' asked Jellicoe, moving on from the subject of his father-in-law.

'Looks like Doney.'

Jellicoe stood beside Culver to inspect the photo. He nodded his head.

'That was my thought.'

'Where are you staying?' asked Culver.

'Grand Flora.'

This made the diminutive American laugh before he replied, 'Nice and handy.' He studied the photograph a little longer then he said, 'Can I keep this?'

'Be my guest. I have a few of them now. Is there anyone else I can speak to who might be able to help me?'

The American answered immediately, 'Paolo Nesta. He writes about crime in the paper. Good guy. Keeps asking me to join him. I can't be bothered. Crime reporters occasionally disappear. I'll stick to obits. I've written three of them for people like Paolo. I'll tell him to expect a call from you.' Culver scribbled down a number for Jellicoe to reach him.

'I'm sure he finds your reason very reassuring,' said Jellicoe. 'Anyone else? For example, where might I find this guy Meazza?'

'Stay in Café de Paris or Harry's Bar long enough and you'll meet them all Nick. They're new and they're hot. All of the great and the good and the very bad go there. There's a guy even making a movie about them. Just follow all the photographers and you'll know where to go.'

Jellicoe ginned and said, 'It's a dirty job but...'

Culver laughed mirthlessly, 'Yeah, yeah, Nick.

They moved away from the topic of the photo while Culver updated Jellicoe on his life in Rome. He was now married, and a child was on the way. The last few months had been quiet on the news front. He told them all he knew about the film being made by Federico Fellini set on the street where Jellicoe and Burnett were staying, Via Veneto.

'You might run into him. He uses the hotel as an office ,' said Culver as he drank some tea. He made a face and looked at Jellicoe accusingly. 'I still don't know how you prefer this muck to coffee.'

'Try with milk,' suggested Burnett sourly. He was enjoying his cuppa and half a dozen sandwiches.

When they'd finished, Jellicoe insisted on picking up the tab which met with an argument from Culver, but he acceded when he heard about his friend's recent inheritance. They parted outside in the piazza.

'I'll see you later. Maybe have more to tell you,' said the American before speeding off on his Vespa, narrowly avoiding sending an aged nun closer to God. She let forth a volley of abuse that was unlikely to have been picked up in the convent. Burnett looked on impressed. He made a mental note to quiz Jellicoe on what she'd said and the accompanying hand gestures.

'Where to now?' asked Burnett. His face was red, and he was visibly wilting in the hot sun.

In truth, Jellicoe was finding the heat stultifying also. It had been an early start. He needed to rest. He said, 'Let's go back to the hotel and have a rest. We have long night ahead of us.'

10

When the two policemen returned to the hotel there were a few large packages wrapped in paper laid out on the two beds. This brought a frown from the older man as he picked up one of the packages. He tore open the paper. Inside was a black dinner suit.

'Bloody hell,' said Burnett.

'Try it on,' suggested Jellicoe.

'For me?'

'Who else?'

Burnett tried to hide his delight but failed signally. Moments later he was tearing off his new suit.

'I could get used to you being rich.'

Jellicoe was rather enjoying the feeling also but another part of him felt a stab of guilt. He was wealthy now, but it was a result of a death. Whatever had become of their marriage, she deserved better than what had happened. It's what she would have wanted, isn't that what they say? Not Sylvia. She was made for life, not for death. Jellicoe shrugged off the morbid thoughts that soon began to engulf him and stared at a rather large butterfly in the shape of the chief inspector emerging from its chrysalis. Burnett now had his new dinner suit and was standing in front of a full-length mirror admiring himself.

'You ordered this n' all?'

'Yes. I knew we'd need it for where we're going over the next few nights.'

Burnett turned one way and then the other. He seemed rather pleased with what he saw.

'Do you think this makes me look like Burt Lancaster?'

'Elsa Lancaster more like.'

'Who's she?' asked Burnett, only half listening.

'The bride of Frankenstein.'

Burnett ignored him and continued to admire himself in the mirror. 'Tell you what, Elsie wouldn't believe what she's seeing here.'

Jellicoe glanced sharply at the chief. He wondered if the man was secretly carrying a deep sense of humiliation and pain at losing his beloved wife.

'Are you sure you're all right?' asked Jellicoe. 'You've mentioned Elsie a few times. Perhaps you should be back home trying to win her back.'

Burnett turned and stared in astonishment at Jellicoe.

'Don't be soft. I'm having fun. I want us to catch this man, Nick, and do you know what? We're going to. Right, when do we go out?'

'In three hours, chief. Get some sleep. You're going to need it.'

*

A few hours later the two men walked into the restaurant of the Grand Flora. Both were dressed in dinner suits. It was now just after seven in the evening, still relatively early for the locals. The restaurant was empty except for one man at another table. There was paper strewn all over the table. The man kept running his hand through his dark hair and shaking his head. A waiter smiled at the two men and showed them to a table on the other side of the restaurant.

'I wonder what's up with him?' murmured Burnett as they sat down. He picked up the menu. His eyes widened.

Jellicoe saw his reaction and smiled. He said, 'I'll tell you what the dishes are.'

'I know what the bloody dishes are, it's the bloody price of them.'

Burnett had a point but Jellicoe, for the moment, no longer cared. As much as the inquest had been a relief to him, a great weight yanked from his shoulders, it had brought back much of the sadness he'd felt. Or was it guilt? Guilt and sadness coexist in grief. The things that were said, or not said; what we did, what we should have done. For too long in their marriage Jellicoe had hated Sylvia. The only person he'd hated more was himself. For staying and putting up with the humiliation. Now he was free in so many senses: free from the fear of jail, free of financial worry, free to find love.

For the first time he realised there was a headiness to how he was reacting. Jellicoe knew this happiness would be short-lived if it did not also bring with it a sense of responsibility. He had to find the man that killed Sylvia. He owed this to her, to her mother, Claudia. Most of all he owed it to himself. He was still Catholic enough to accept that this was his penance.

'What do you recommend?' asked Burnett. Despite his rather blunt manner, he was known to have an appreciation of food that his girth only barely alluded to. Jellicoe suggested the Amatriciana while he had Parmigiana. Rather than order a bottle for wine, Jellicoe suggested they just confine themselves to one glass each. This was brought a growl from Burnett who'd had his eyes on a Montepulciano.

While they waited for their meal, Burnett eyed Jellicoe.

'Who were you calling earlier?'

'Sorry, did I wake you?'

'No, I was only dozing.'

'I've arranged to meet Paolo Nesta, the crime reporter Culver mentioned. We're meeting him at eight thirty at the Café de Paris. He speaks English you'll be glad to hear.'

An hour later they finished their meal and Burnett looked on with a broad grin as Jellicoe settled up.

'I could watch you doing that all day long,' observed Burnett with a cackle.

As they walked out of the restaurant, he took a pipe out of his pocket. Jellicoe looked quietly stupefied.

'What?' asked Burnett, a little hurt by Jellicoe's reaction to the pipe.

'It's fine out here, but please don't bring it out when we're in the nightclubs. Do you smoke?'

'Never really liked it,' admitted Burnett, lighting the pipe. 'Anyway, it helps me think.'

'Just not in the nightclub.'

'All right,' said Burnett, sounding once more like a child in a sulk.

It was twilight hour in Rome. Via Veneto traffic was building, car lights on but the sky overhead was mauve. Burnett gazed up awestruck at the starlings in the sky. They were flying in formations that would have had a British Army drill sergeant taking notes.

'Amazing aren't they,' said Jellicoe noting the direction of Burnett's gaze.

'How do they do it?'

'Oh, birds are like detectives. They'll always follow a good leader,' said Jellicoe drily.

'I wonder how our beloved leader, Widow Twanky is coping without his top men,' laughed Burnett. He was still puffing contentedly on his pipe. The pipe presented quite a contrast with the Brioni dinner suit that, for once, made Burnett look quite sharply dressed. Burnett caught Jellicoe looking at the pipe.

'Aye I'll get a move on, but we've time yet.'

'We do, confirmed Jellicoe. 'The nightclub is just down the road from here.' Silence fell between them, as the two men returned to marvelling at the astonishing show taking place in the sky.

Soon though the show in the sky began to take second place to the floor show on Via Veneto. It began when Burnett accidentally bumped into a young woman. He apologised and then realised she was the most beautiful woman he had ever seen. Her claim to the title lasted barely a minute as Burnett studied the parade of young women on the street with an increasing sense of delight.

'Tell you what, Nick. These Italian lasses aren't half all right.'

Jellicoe had noted the same thing and the two men strolled happily along the street towards their destination.

'I think we'll sit outside,' said Jellicoe, eyeing a few empty seats outside the bar. The two men sat down allowing them a perfect view of the passing beauty parade of expensively clad young women and pomaded young men, gigolos and at least one man that Burnett recognised but could not put a name to.

'He was in that film,' said Burnett to Jellicoe who had only seen the back of the man in question.

'Which film?'

'You know it.'

'I really don't.'

Burnett clicked his finger a few times in an effort to try and remember. All it succeeded in doing was offending the waiter who thought Burnett was trying to attract his attention. He wandered pouting.

'It's not you,' said Jellicoe in Italian. 'He's trying to remember the name of the actor that just passed us.'

The light of forgiveness shone from the waiter's eyes as well as recognition.

'Stephen Boyd,' said the waiter.

Burnett snapped his fingers again, 'That's the fella.'

They ordered a bottle of white wine and waited for someone approximating the appearance of Paolo Nesta to arrive.

'Does he look like Santa Claus on a diet?' asked Burnett a few minutes later.

Jellicoe turned in the direction Burnett was facing and saw a tall, strongly built man approach. More Hemingway than Father Christmas but close enough. He waved to the man, who smiled and waved back. His teeth shone brightly against his dark, weathered skin.

'Mr Jellicoe?' asked the man. Unlike them, he was dressed very much in the manner of an American college professor of American history who is a secret Anglophile but cannot bring himself to admit it. He sported an old Harris Tweed jacket and grey cotton trousers with brown brogues. Jellicoe and Burnett stood up and shook hands with the crime reporter. While Burnett filled his glass, Jellicoe explained the reason for their visit. He took a copy of the photograph Claudia had given him out of his breast pocket and handed it to the Italian.

'The lady to the right is my wife, Sylvia. She was murdered last year in London. The man to the left is her father, my father-in-law. Culver thought that you might know these men. He didn't say anything about them, but I know Culver. I think they may be involved in crime.'

This brought a smile from the Italian, and he handed the photograph back to Jellicoe.

'You don't want to keep it?' asked Jellicoe, a little disappointed.

'I don't need to. I know these men, and Culver is correct. They are involved in crime. Very involved.'

Jellicoe exhaled slowly and glanced at Burnett whose eyes had widened at this exchange.

'Who are they?

'I'm sorry to hear of your loss,' said Nesta and appeared to mean it. 'The man beside your father is Giovanni Lentini. He owns a number of businesses, in particular several car dealerships. He is suspected of being involved in money laundering for major crime bosses. You know, washing their money clean.'

Jellicoe nodded.

'Of course, it is difficult to prove all this, and our police force are very undermanned.' This last point was made with more than a trace of cynicism.

'I know the feeling,' said Burnett bitterly.

'A common problem I see,' said Nesta shaking his head.

'The man on the other side of your wife is Matteo de Luca. This is a very bad man. You should be careful with this one. Again we have no proof, but I can categorically say that he is a major supplier of drugs in Rome, particularly to the idle rich. I am sure there is much blood on his hands. The young man beside him,' Nesta paused for a moment. There could be no doubt that the young man in question and Jellicoe's wife were on intimate terms. He glanced carefully at Jellicoe.

'My wife and I were close to separating when she was murdered,' explained Jellicoe with a shrug. This was probably a lie but what else could he say? Even to think of how he had turned a blind eye to her infidelity hurt him still long after he'd ceased to care about her or what she'd done. It was his virtual submission to her infidelity at the time in return for the gilded life he was leading that hurt.

'I see. This is Lorenzo de Luca. He is the son of Matteo. They say he is being made ready to take over the business from his father. Matteo is my age, sixty-five. I hear he wants to step away from day to day running of his companies and give it to his son. Like most father's he is a little blind. I understand that the Matteo is a just a playboy. Smart but very immature. Anyway these are the men that your wife and father-in-law where with that night.'

'Thanks,' said Jellicoe and turned to Burnett. 'What do you think, chief?'

Burnett looked hard at Jellicoe before replying, 'Same as you son. Just what was your wife and father-in-law doing with people like this?' Jellicoe smiled mirthlessly and nodded. What indeed? Burnett wasn't finished.

'Just what line of business was your father-in-law in?' asked Burnett, helping himself and the others to a little more wine. He drained the bottle and held it up to the waiter hopefully.

'He imported antique furniture from Europe.'

Silence fell over the table as they considered the implications of this. Jellicoe felt the weight return. The repercussions of this conversation were almost too much to bear. Nesta could see the impact on Jellicoe and felt a wave of sympathy towards the policeman that surprised him. He and the chief were massively out of their depth. He decided that it was for him to confirm the thought that he could clearly on their faces.

'I think Mr Jellicoe, this something you should hand over to the police here and with your own Scotland Yard. I don't doubt you and Mr Burnett's capabilities, but you are swimming in deep waters here.'

'What do you think is happening here?' asked Jellicoe, gazing at the smiling Sylvia. For the first time he turned his attention to other people in the photograph, standing behind the table. It was conceivable that they were all part of the same party. The photograph was cropped half way up their bodies so it was not possible to see any faces, but it was clear that by the stouter shapes of the men and the slender bodies of the women what was going on because all around them they could see the same story playing out on Via Veneto.

Nesta fixed his eyes on Jellicoe and breathed heavily. Then he spoke. He put his elbows on the table, removed his glasses and rubbed his eyes. He replaced the glasses and took out some cigarettes. He offered them to Jellicoe and Burnett, but they shook their heads.

'Have you heard about the Montesi case?' he asked the two English policemen.

11

'Look around you,' began Nesta. 'Via Veneto is a Mecca now for the rich and famous in Rome. Beautiful girls, young men, old men, film stars, criminals all come here and do what we are doing. Here you are not judged if you are rich. Crime bosses mix freely, sleep with and drink with the stars. No one cares anymore. This is Sodom and Gomorrah rolled into one and that man over there, is making a film about it.'

Nesta pointed to a man who had just arrived and was led to a seat by a man dressed in a suit who appeared to be like a host in the bar rather than one of the waiters.

'That's the lad who was in the restaurant with us earlier,' pointed out Burnett.

The lad in questions was a man in his thirties, a little bit stout with thick dark hair slicked back from his forehead.

'Federico Fellini,' said Nesta, 'do you know of him?'

Nesta may as well have been talking about nuclear fusion to Burnett. Jellicoe just nodded.

'I saw La Strada and Nights of Cabiria.'

Nesta seemed oddly impressed by this but continued with the story he wanted to tell.

'His new film is about life here on this street, but I can tell you it is about something else to.'

'The Montesi case?' asked Burnett.

'Yes. The Montesi case. Wilma Montesi was a young girl, a beautiful young girl I should say, just like the ones you see around you. She came from a good family, good Catholic girl. Obedient, quiet a daughter to be proud of yet she ended up dead on a beach. Murdered. How did she, this good Catholic girl, end up on a beach, dressed like a Hollywood star, far from home? She died in 1953 and yet here we are six years later, and we still have no idea who killed her, why she was there. There have been court cases, theories, witnesses, suspects, you can read about them in the scandal rags.'

'But what has this to do with our case?' pressed Burnett.

'Everything, my friend. You see Wilma Montesi was involved with rich men, the sons of politicians like Piero Piccioni, with criminals like Ugo Montagna. She was like a moth flying to close to the flame. Drugs. This is the blight which is taking over the cities. It will only become worse. Men like Montagna and the men in your photograph are supplying these drugs to their rich clients. Young women like Wilma Montesi were like couriers. One day, and it will be sooner than you think, drugs will no longer just be the preserve of the idle rich. When it reaches the poor we will be in trouble.'

Jellicoe could barely touch his drink as he listened to more details about the case from the journalist. When Nesta had finished he turned to Burnett. There was bitterness in his voice.

'Chief, I don't think this is a good idea. You shouldn't be here. I'm not sure I should be here. It's not your fight.'

Burnett's eyes blazed at Jellicoe. He was not angry at him so much as what he had been hearing about.

'A week. We'll give this a week and see who we can upset.'

Jellicoe nodded and returned his gaze to the crime reporter.

'Well, we're not exactly the US cavalry but we're going to ruffle some feathers if we can. Sylvia deserves that at least. So does this young girl you spoke of.'

Nesta shook his head in frustration.

'Culver thinks that you're a good policeman, but you have to be realistic. You are going up against organised crime. We have a police force, a highly capable police force, I might add who, with greater resources, with local knowledge, with many contacts have made little or no progress against these people. How do you expect to achieve anything beyond putting your lives at risk?'

It was a pertinent question to which neither man had an answer. Jellicoe admitted as much but it was clear to Nesta that this was unlikely to put the two men off. Nesta shrugged. It was their time. Their life. He looked to change the subject.

'Has anyone ever told you, Mr Jellicoe, that you...'

'Here we go...' interrupted Burnett.

Jellicoe grinned and nodded, 'Yes, it has been said.' He was referring to the resemblance to the Rome-based English actor, Anthony Steel.

'His wife is making the film with our friend Fellini over there. I wonder if that's why he has been looking at you strangely.'

'We saw him at the Grand Flora restaurant earlier,' replied Jellicoe.

Fellini had been joined by another man now. A short man of a similar age.

'Ahh, Victor,' said Nesta, nodding a hello to the new arrival. The new arrival smiled back at Nesta and then his brow took on the shape of corrugated metal as he looked at Jellicoe.

'You had better get used to this Mr Jellicoe,' whispered Nesta.

At this point, the man named Victor waved for Nesta and the two policemen to come over.

'Shall we?' asked Nesta.

'I'd love to meet Fellini,' responded Jellicoe.

'Who?' asked Burnett but Jellicoe could see the smile behind the eyes.

The three men rose from their seats and walked over to the table where Fellini and Victor were sitting. Nesta appeared to know Fellini as the two men embraced warmly.

'Gentlemen,' said Nesta in Italian, 'May I introduce Nick Jellicoe and Reg Burnett. From England. This is Federico Fellini our foremost film director and Victor Ciuffa, a colleague on the Corriere d'Informazione.'

In fact, Victor Ciuffa was the gossip columnist on the newspaper and would soon become famous as the man who Fellini would played by Marcello Mastroianni in the film he was making.

As they shook hands Jellicoe noted the smile on Fellini's face. Nesta spoke rapidly to Fellini to tell him that the policeman was aware of the resemblance to the husband of his leading actress.

'What brings you to Roma? 'asked Ciuffa in heavily accented English, inviting the men to join them with a wave of his hand. He sensed there was an interesting story. The question made Nesta both smile and frown. He knew what the little gossip columnist was asking – why are two British policemen having a drink with Rome's foremost crime reporter? Nesta thought to intervene but remained silent.

Jellicoe replied in Italian, 'I have come to find my wife's killer.'

Burnett could guess what his detective inspector had said by the reaction of the two Italians they'd been introduced to. First, there was acknowledgement that the Englishman could speak Italian. This was unusual. The English, in the two men's experience, had little aptitude never mind enthusiasm for speaking anything other than their own language. Their arrogance in assuming that everyone should speak their language was too often justified as the world was forced to do so anyway thanks to the enormous economic power wielded by the United States.

The expression on their faces changed rapidly as they digested what the policeman had said. They turned immediately to a resigned-looking Nesta. Jellicoe wasn't sure if admitting the reason for their visit was a good thing or not, but he felt the gamble was worth it. He wanted the men involved with Sylvia's death to know he was coming whatever the risk. However, he would speak once more to Burnett. He would not countenance the idea of putting his chief's life at risk.

Nesta shrugged and explained rapidly the background to the two men's presence in Rome. Fellini and Ciuffa were fascinated. In for a penny, thought Jellicoe. He took the photograph out of his pocket and showed it to the two men.

'She's beautiful,' murmured Fellini as Jellicoe pointed to his wife. 'My condolences.'

It was obvious that he did not know the other men and equally obvious that Ciuffa did. He stared hard at Nesta as if warning him to reveal who the men were and why it was not a good idea to be doing what the Englishmen proposed. Nesta shrugged.

'I told them,' said Nesta resignedly.

This brought a frown from the gossip columnist. Just as he was about to say something on this subject a scooter pulled up alongside them on the road. Two men were on the scooter. One of them was clutching a camera. He took a photograph of the group, blinding them with the flash from the camera.

Ciuffa leased off a volley of insults, but it was clear he was laughing more than angry. The scooter tore off into the night.

'Friend of yours?' asked Jellicoe, smiling. He had seen these photographers in the past. They patrolled Via Veneto and the nightclubs like an army of mosquitoes. Their target was the rich and famous, their market was gossip columnists like Victor Ciuffa and the many scandal magazines that were bought from the roadside newspaper kiosks in their tens of thousands.

Jellicoe took his cue from Nesta on when they should leave. It came a couple of minutes later and they rose from the table with handshakes all around. As they left, Jellicoe noted that Nesta and Ciuffa exchanged a quiet word with one another. Nesta re-joined them but remained standing as the two policemen took their seats.

'I must leave you now. I hope I have helped you.'

'You have,' said Jellicoe.

'May I appeal to you once more. Leave this alone. I think you are placing yourselves in danger if you pursue this too much. I have a friend in the police force, Commisario Fausto Conti. Give him the photograph and tell him what you know. He can help you.'

Nesta knew his plea would fall on deaf ears just as Jellicoe knew that this man Conti would know before the night was out that two English policemen were embarking on a Quixotic adventure to find the killer of an Anglo-Italian woman in London.

When Nesta had departed, Burnett returned to the wine with the enthusiastic observation that there was more for them to share now that the Italian was gone.

'What did you make of him?' asked Burnett.

'I liked him. He has a point though, Chief.'

'You mean we are taking a few risks here,' replied Burnett before downing half a glass of the wine.

'Yes. Look, I really think you should go back,' said Jellicoe. There was a seriousness in his tone that made Burnett stop mid drink, never a good idea.

'I can take care of myself, son. Discussion over, all right?'

So that was that. Burnett was going nowhere. Whether this was a risk to Jellicoe or a benefit he was not sure. Burnett was a first-class detective and a shrewd judge of character. Furthermore, he had a practical side to him that meant he honed in on the key friction points in a case and worried less about psychology and motive. Means and opportunity guided him more than speculating about whys and wherefores. Motive had its place, of course, but more often than not, cases were solved through basic policework which involved cross checking alibis, and anything and everything to do with the means by which murder was committed: the capability if the individual and their access to a murder weapon. Find the answers to these and you were usually there or thereabouts in finding the murderer.

'So, Sherlock. Where do we start?'

'I think you'll like the answer.'

'What's that?'

'A bar.'

12

'First time I've ever done a pub crawl and called it a murder investigation,' said Burnett gleefully. This was partly prompted by the thrill of the chase, the heady feeling of being in the world's most beautiful city and wholly by the bottle of wine he'd consumed at the Café de Paris. A man could grow to love Italy, he thought and then another ravishing beauty passed him walking hand in hand with an older gentleman. Yes, a man could get used to this. Jellicoe and Burnett were walking back up via Veneto towards the Grand Flora hotel. Their destination was Harry's Bar which was opposite where they were staying on the corner of the road facing the ancient Roman wall and Villa Borghese. It was night time now. The lights of open-topped cars and the sound of horns filled the air.

'These Italians aren't very patient,' observed Burnett as yet another car was on the receiving end of a several sharp blasts of car horns for committing the hanging offence of stopping at a red traffic light. Italians used the lights more for guidance than strict observance. Jellicoe looked at the chief inspector archly but said nothing.

'What?' exclaimed Burnett, 'You saying I'm impatient? Cheeky git.'

They came to a stop outside the bar. Originally opened by an American lady who named it 'Golden Gate', it had been renamed in the fifties, possibly in response to the news that the Harry's Bar in Venice was a favourite of Ernest Hemingway. The one in Rome soon proved to be a popular haunt, like the Café de Paris, for celebrities, politicians and the rich. Outside the door was a pack of photographers including the little man that had snapped him and Burnett with Fellini and Victor Ciuffa.

The man in question was short dressed in a rumpled suit. He eyed the approaching Jellicoe closely then put the camera before putting it down again and frowning. Jellicoe smiled at his confusion.

'Non sono Anthony Steel,' said Jellicoe (I'm not Anthony Steel) as he passed him. He felt a tug on his arm.

'Who are you?' asked the man.

Jellicoe considered ignoring him but then a thought struck him. He stopped and spoke again to the little man in Italian, 'Nick Jellicoe.' Then he fished out the photograph of Sylvia in the night club. He turned it around and showed the photographer the name on the back.

'Where can I find this man?' asked Jellicoe.

The photographer smiled and showed the name to the other photographers waiting outside Harry's Bar. Then he turned the photograph around and looked at the people. His expression changed immediately.

'Who are you?' asked the man.

'I told you. Who are you?' asked Jellicoe.

'Geno. Geno Muro,' came the answer. 'What are these people to you?'

'One of them is my wife. I want to meet the others and the man that took this picture.'

Muro made a gesture with his hand which Jellicoe interpreted to mean that he thought this was not a great idea.

'Do you know who these men are?' asked Muro.

Jellicoe nodded but pressed on, 'Where can I find them?'

Behind him Burnett was listening without understanding much of what was going on.

'Hurry up son. There's a drink with my name on it in here.'

'Meet me tomorrow,' said Muro.

'Where?'

'Il Baretto, Via del Babuino. Do you know it?'

Il Baretto was a popular bar on the street leading towards the Spanish Steps. Unlike Via Veneto, which was popular with the rich and famous, the area around Via Marguta, a narrow street near the Spanish Steps, was a different world, a focal point for artists and bohemians. Jellicoe knew it well because he and Sylvia had been there many times.

'Tomorrow, one o'clock,' said Muro.

It would cost him a lunch, but he had the money now. Or did he? The thought of his new found wealth had suddenly a little less reassuring. He had been rich for a week and already he was unhappy. Who says money buys happiness he thought? In the past, his view of people who complained about wealth was distinctly unsympathetic. To be rich and unhappy was a failure of the imagination. Yet here he was feeling the very thing that he'd dismissed so readily in others. They shook hands to seal the meeting then they entered Harry's Bar and made straight for the first free table that they could find.

'This looks like the place the photograph was taken,' observed Burnett.

'Yes,' agreed, Jellicoe. He pointed to a table a few feet away. A chill descended on him as he thought about the moment that his wife would have been here. He remembered the trip now. She and her parents had gone to Rome just before Christmas in 1957. He had been working on a murder in outside London. They had gone away for a week. They did this several times a year. Sometimes he would accompany them, often not. I want to see my family, Sylvia would say. Stephen said it was for business. What type of business though? Were Lentini and the de Luca's business partners?

While Jellicoe was lost in these thoughts he was only vaguely aware that Burnett, whose Italian had improved with every glass of wine was ordering the same bottle of Asti Spumante that he'd spotted a woman drinking on a nearby table. When the bottle arrived Burnett raised his glass to the woman who looked to be in her late fifties. She was dressed younger than was probably sensible, but she was attractive and happily reciprocated Burnett's toast.

'Steady on Romeo,' said Jellicoe to his chief.

'Just being friendly,' replied Burnett. He began to scan the room. 'Any sign of the men in the picture?'

'No, but I wasn't expecting to see them. For all I know they may be at the coast. The locals tend to leave Rome during August. It's too hot.'

'They're not wrong there. So what are we doing here then?'

It was a fair question, a simple one even but without an obvious answer. Jellicoe wanted to be in the places that Sylvia had been. He wanted to step into the black and white photograph immerse himself in the atmosphere, observe the people, understand the rules of engagement. What he learned tonight simply drinking with Burnett would not feel much explicitly but it would be more implicitly than he knew the previous day, and now, he was glad to have Burnet with him.

He didn't know why but something inside him suggested he would have his role in this tragedy or farce. Life usually ended up as one or the other.

Jellicoe sipped the Spumante and immediately wondered how much it was going to cost him. The bubbles slowly worked their magic and he realised he no longer cared.

'We've already accomplished something,' answered Jellicoe.

'Go on,' said Burnett leaning forward. He was rather impressive in his own way, thought Jellicoe. They had both had quite a lot to drink already and it seemed to have had no effect on him apart from a slight lightening of his mood.

'We know who we want to speak to now and tomorrow perhaps we'll find out how and where this will be possible.'

Burnett seemed unimpressed by this. With good reason too, accepted Jellicoe. Yet this was only part of the object for which he was striving. The other was an idea, not yet fully formed, that the whoever killed or Sylvia or, at least, ordered her death, should know that he was coming for him. The latter point had grown in his mind since finding out who the other men in the picture were. The murder of Sylvia could either be seen as the random act of a psychopath or, and this was new, a deliberate act within the context of some unknown, undeclared gang war. The underlying assumption was that Stephen was involved in smuggling drugs. Jellicoe felt pretty confident that this was this case.

'I'm sure these criminal masterminds will be happy to speak to you,' said Burnett sarcastically. 'A few questions from supersleuth Jellicoe and they'll crumble. They'll confess everything they've done since they first stole sweets from the sweetshop.'

'What do you think then?'

'What do I think? I think we'll have to give this another day or two here, in the meantime I would get Scotland Yard onto your mother-in-law or, better still, get them going through every piece of paper that your father-in law has, private and business to find a trail that leads to where we both think it leads.'

'Importing drugs.'

Burnett nodded at this but said nothing. He glanced down at the Spumante before adding, 'I could get used to this, I could.'

'Don't let it go to your head.'

'I could say the same to you, son. There's only so far we can take this before we'll have to pass it on. What did you say to the little photographer?'

Jellicoe told him about the meeting. Then he sat back and wondered what Muro would be able to do for him. The photographers and their quarry, the film stars, the politicians, the playboys, the models had a symbiotic relationship. They needed one another. There was a growing demand for magazines like Confidential, that Jellicoe had seen in the US, that exploited the scandals of the rich and famous that walked a fine line between morality and obscenity. The magazines sold in their thousands as the public devoured tales of wild parties, illicit affairs and badly behaved public figures.

People like Victor Ciuffa were of the old school. The new and aggressive intrusiveness of these magazines shattered the gently conservative social diaries that were a fixture in all of the newspapers and replaced them with sensationalism, conjecture and a cheerfully anti-establishment stance that had the government, the judiciary and the church running scared.

The more Jellicoe thought about the matter the more another question rose in his mind. A question that he found as extraordinary as it was unanswerable now.

Who was Sylvia?

13

Hotel Grand Flora, Rome: 21st August 1959

The shrill ring of the phone sliced through Jellicoe's senses forcing his eyes open. The room was dark and nearby it sounded like there was Yak snorting in the throes of conjugal bliss. Still the phone persisted in competing against the in inhuman noise creating an unholy cacophony that made Jellicoe want to shout.

And then things began to spin. It might have been the room or his head, but it was all damned confusing. Instinctively, his arm struck out the in the direction of the ringing. It encountered the source of the racket piercing very mind. He lifted the receiver and then put it down again. All at once the ring stopped. Unfortunately, the snoring did not. With an effort of will Jellicoe rose like Frankenstein's monster to address the second obstruction to his overwhelming need to sleep. Just as he did this, the phone blasted its strident message, answer me, answer me. Reluctantly, Jellicoe swung around and picked up the phone.

'Yes, who is it?' he said in a hoarse whisper that he barely recognised as his own voice.

'Hey Nick, it's Culver.'

'What do you want? What time is it?'

His mind was clogged by alcohol and memories of the previous night. Somewhere in the fog he could see Burnett doing a rumba while he was smoking a pipe. He'd never smoked a pipe before. His tongue felt like it had been coated with sewage.

'What did you guys get up to last night? You're all over the papers.'

'I'm what?' groaned Jellicoe but his mind was quickly snapping back to life. 'What do you mean?'

'You and the chief are in a couple of the papers. In one of them they're quoting you saying that you have come to find your wife's killer.'

Well, in a manner of speaking he had achieved what he'd wanted. Perhaps though his ploy had proved a little more successful than he'd either planned or wanted. It was one thing to shake the tree a little, it was another to set fire to it and to yourself in the process. He needed time to think through the implications of what he was hearing in a quiet place and sober fashion.

Sober.

'What does it say?'

Culver started laughing and began to read.

'English detective Nick Jellicoe is over to investigate the murder of his wife. Jellicoe, who bears an amazing resemblance to English actor, Anthony Steel, is pictured here dancing the night away at Bricktops near Via Veneto. The English detective presents an unusual contrast with the traditional image we have of sleuths from this country. Sherlock Holmes must be spinning in his fictional grave.'

'Oh God,' said Jellicoe running a hand through his hair. It was wet. He put his hand to his nose. He could smell alcohol.

In fact as his sense of smell began to wake up, he realised two things. He could smell a lot of alcohol and, more disconcertingly, he was still dressed in his dinner suit.

'Nick, I have to tell you, when the scandal rags see this, they'll be following you all over Rome. I can just see it: good looking English cop out to avenge his wife's murder by partying like a playboy. Man they're going to love you.'

'Great,' said Jellicoe without much enthusiasm. In the bed next to his, the snoring had stopped. Burnett, too, was fully clothed, splayed out on the bed like a Wile E. Coyote after he has fallen from a cliff. This gave Jellicoe pause to smile but the pounding in his head soon wiped any enjoyment of the moment away.

'Did you meet Paolo?'

'Yeah, I did. Good guy,' said Jellicoe and meant it. However, a thought strayed unbidden in his head. 'Which newspaper did you say this was in?'

There was a pause on the line. If embarrassment had a sound it was probably something like this.

'I had nothing to do with this Nick.'

'The Corriere, then?'

'Yes,' admitted Culver.

'It wasn't a Victor Ciuffa who wrote this by any chance?'

'Yes, Nick. Nice shot of you and him together along with Federico Fellini. You get around old pal.'

'Tell me about it. The shots of us dancing. That was a lot later in the evening.'

'That's pretty obvious by the look on your faces and the way you're dressed.'

'Great. Thanks Culver. Anything else?'

'Well, I suppose one thing occurs to me.'

106

'Expect the police to be in touch, you mean?'

Culver laughed and then became more serious, 'You're a good cop Nick. That much is obvious. I wonder how much of this was on your mind when you went around telling everyone what you were doing. None of my business but listen. Be careful old pal. These are dangerous people.'

'So I gather. I'll take care. Thanks Culver,' said Jellicoe ringing off. The call confirmed one suspicion that had been hanging over him. Culver had known who the men were in the picture, yet he'd effectively delegated it to Paolo Nesta to tell him. This had suited Jellicoe, but it made him wonder why he had not come out with it when they met.

One thing was certain: the police would be in touch soon. Moreover, if he were to place a bet on which policeman it would be, his money was on the man Nesta had mentioned the previous evening, Commisario Conti.

Jellicoe was now, in a manner of speaking, awake. There was nothing for it but to prepare himself for the meeting that was not so much looming as hurtling towards him like a runaway train. He made it to the bathroom without falling flat on his face.

The bathroom light revealed his face in all of its splendour. He looked in the mirror, still drunk from his all night, binge with Burnett. In the harsh light of the bathroom, the dark circles under his eyes resembled nothing less than those of a dissolute panda. He threw cold water over his face then ran the bath. If he weren't feeling well then the least he could do was to look the part of an English gentleman. The clank and rattle of Burnett's snoring resumed in the bedroom.

How many hours sleep had they had? It was nine now. He remembered staggering through the lobby of the hotel around five in the morning. Four hours sleep? He'd survived on less before but perhaps not with the amount of wine and champagne he'd shipped the previous evening.

Twenty minutes later he'd washed and shaved. He felt a little bit better now. He wondered how Burnett would be. Jellicoe's drinking had been the very personification of moderation in comparison to the chief. It was as if he'd been set free after a long sentence served in a prison called Temperance. Jellicoe stared at the inert figure of Burnett and wondered how he would ever recover from the previous evening. It was time to find out. He stepped forward and threw open the curtains. Light flooded into the room.

Burnett remained unconscious.

Next, Jellicoe went to the radio and switched it on. He moved the dial away from a news programme to music. A female voice. It sounded familiar. He turned the volume dial up to its maximum point.

'Nessuno, ti giuro, nessuno,' sang the woman. It was a rock n' roll song. He quite liked the raw power of this. Despite the best efforts of the singer, her vocal efforts were ineffective against the thunderous machine gun rattle of Burnett's snoring. The choice between effecting a Lazarus-like raising of the dead, or leaving him be, was not a difficult one. In fact, through the murkiness of his mind at that moment, Jellicoe saw some benefits to Burnett remaining in the background.

Dressed, washed and shaved, Jellicoe looked presentable even if he did not feel it. He closed the curtains again, switched off the radio before exiting the room. He went downstairs and made straight for the reception.

'I am expecting a visit from the police this morning,' he announced to the rather startled man on reception. Jellicoe smiled, 'It's nothing to worry about. I'm just going around the corner for a coffee to Bar Veneto. Can you send them there and say I am expecting them.'

'Yes Mr Jellicoe, and your friend?'

'Mr Burnett is still sleeping. It was a late night. If he does come down, and I very much doubt that he will, please send him to Bar Veneto also.

Jellicoe ambled out onto Via Veneto. He was a little steadier on his feet and perhaps with the assistance of an espresso or three he would re-join the world in some sort of fettle. He walked around the corner to the bar and ordered an espresso with a cornetto before sitting outside at a table for four. He wondered how long he would have to wait before his guests arrived.

Twenty minutes later he spied two men walking towards the bar with purposeful strides and a look of determination in their eyes. As they drew closer, Jellicoe re-evaluated his assessment and decided their expression was anger. Fair enough. He would be angry too if some foreign detectives came to his town and embarked on a unilateral investigation of Ronnie Musgrave or Johnny Warwick, the local gang leaders.

One of the men was around Jellicoe's age, tall, slender with a thin moustache and a cigarette dangling from his mouth like James Dean. The older man was an Italian version of Burnett. He had the appearance of an American Pit Bull and if the expression on his face was any guide, he had just about as much of that canine's gentle, serene nature. Jellicoe's eyes met those of the older man. Jellicoe smiled in greeting which made the man's countenance darken significantly. Jellicoe rose as they neared the table. He held his hand out and gambled with his opening.

'Commisario Conti, I presume,' said Jellicoe in Italian.

This was met with a scowl; the handshake was ignored. They all stood for a moment then Jellicoe held his hand out.

'Let me organise some coffees. Can I tempt you with a brioche.'

The silence which greeted this suggested the next few minutes would be interesting. Jellicoe caught the eye of the barista and gestured for three more coffees.

'Let's sit down,' said Jellicoe. 'I had a rather tiring night.'

Was it his imagination but there seemed to be a softening in the older man's expression. It was momentary, though. The glint returned to his eyes. He spoke in heavily accented English.

'My friend Nesta did not tell me he'd warned you I was coming.'

'He didn't,' replied Jellicoe. 'I guessed when I heard saw the newspaper.' Jellicoe picked up the Corriere.

The frown on Conti's face deepened. He said, 'Let us not play games here Detective Inspector Jellicoe. What do you think you are doing?'

Conti did not seem like a man who could be hoodwinked never mind toyed with. However, full disclosure would probably earn him a one-way ticket back to England. His answer, like all good responses in an interrogation had to be two parts truth and one part evasion.

'I want to find out more about who killed my wife and why. The trail has led me here.'

This did not appear to come close to satisfying the Commisario. He leaned forward, his face twisting into a snarl that Burnett would have been proud of.

'Do not take me for a fool. You should not be here. No police force in the world would sanction one of their officers to investigate a family member's death.'

'I didn't say they had. I've come of my own volition. I don't believe Scotland Yard would approve of my actions and I may face consequences when you undoubtedly tell them but nor can they stop me from doing what I wish on holiday, Commisario. That much you'll have to accept.'

Conti slammed the table causing the cups and saucers to jump off the plates.

'I will not accept a crusade or some vigilante project. You do not know what you are dealing with here.'

'I have some idea Commisario, and I fully intend to continue.'

'Then your stay here will be as short as the rest of your career in the police, Jellicoe,' snapped Conti.

'That's my problem, Commisario. Do as you see fit. I will too.'

Conti's eyes widened at this. Then he rose sharply from his seat. It was as if he did not trust himself to say anything more to the English policeman. There was no goodbye only a promise in the final look that Conti gave Jellicoe.

One way or another, the clock was ticking now on his time in Rome. He would need to work fast as he sensed Conti would act quickly to bring him to heel. He waited until the policemen were out of sight before leaving the bar. He walked quickly back to the hotel powered by the two espressos he'd taken in the bar. As he entered the hotel, he saw what he expected to see. A man in a suit sitting in the lobby reading a newspaper. He wondered if Conti had more men, or did he have similar manpower challenges that they had in Britain.

When he returned to the bedroom he was greeted by the sound of Burnett singing in the bath. Jellicoe wasn't sure which was worse, the snoring or the singing. The song getting the Burnett treatment was 'I Won't Dance'.

A pet hate of Jellicoe's was when people sang a popular standard but contrived to get the lyrics wrong. Burnett was making a rare old mess of the song. Jellicoe shook his head then wandered over to the bed and lay down. He would have given anything to have a few more hours of sleep. Perhaps after lunch. He shut his eyes just to rest them a little.

The next thing he knew he was being shaken awake by Burnett.

'Wakey, wakey son. Rise and shine. We have a lunch appointment.'

'What?' slurred Jellicoe. His eyes began to focus, and he saw Burnett sitting over him with a broad grin on his face.

'Lunch. You said you were meeting that photographer lad, didn't you?'

Jellicoe's mind slowly laboured into gear. This was true but what time was it and how could Burnett be in such good form after seeming so dead to the world earlier. Jellicoe's eyes had cleared sufficiently for him to be able to see his watch. It was twelve thirty. He'd been asleep for two hours.

'Oh,' said Jellicoe.

'Oh indeed,' said Burnett. He picked up the Corriere and opened it up to the page where they both were featuring. 'Have you seen this?' he said bursting out into loud laughter.

'I'd noticed. So have the Italian police, I saw them this morning.'

'I wondered where you'd gone. I suppose we'll be hearing from our lot soon.'

'Count on it,' groaned Jellicoe swinging his long legs off the bed.

'Best get a move on then,' said Burnett. Jellicoe wasn't sure if he was referring to the case or their appointment with Geno Muro.

14

'Have you had breakfast yet? 'asked Jellicoe as he and Burnett exited the hotel. The man from the lobby quickly followed them. He did not seem too concerned about whether or not he was seen. Fair enough, thought Jellicoe: you'll care in a few moments. Jellicoe ignored the groan from Burnett as they walked towards the Vespa parked outside the hotel.

'No, I haven't eaten yet. Is this going to be a long trip?' moaned Burnett.

'No, just a few minutes,' said Jellicoe starting the Vespa.

'Who is our friend over there?' asked Burnett, nodding towards the man Jellicoe had spotted in the lobby.

Jellicoe was oddly impressed that Burnett had seen their shadow. In fact, Burnett appeared to be remarkably unaffected from last night's expedition around the night spots of Via Veneto and if anything was in a good humour. The same could not be said for their shadow who now realised that he had no way of following them. Jellicoe and Burnett both waved to him as they sped off. He waved them off too. With his fist. His volley of abuse was lost in the roar of the Vespa, no, make that buzz.

Burnett kept his eyes firmly shut as they sped down Via Veneto. The journey was as mercifully short as Jellicoe had promised. They drew up to the bar on Via del Babuino. The street was quiet except for a few tourists. Certainly, no one would have followed them. The bar was empty and was just as Jellicoe remembered it: narrow, intimate with cured meat hanging on one wall and shelves full of red wine. Jellicoe thought it looked beautiful, almost like a jewellery shop. He went over to a seat, while Burnett indicated he would go over to the bar and order.

'Watch this,' said Burnett. 'I'm beginning to pick up the lingo.'

Jellicoe watched.

Burnett strode over to the bar like an overweight gunslinger new into town. The barista, a young man with movie star looks raised one eyebrow at the new customer. Burnett glanced over to Jellicoe and winked. He held up two fingers and said, 'Doo-ay Ca-fays por favor.'

Notwithstanding the lapse into Spanish at the end, he appeared to have got the ball over the net. The barista repeated the order before telling Burnett the price. This was a hurdle that the chief inspector had not anticipated. He turned sharply to Jellicoe with a look of alarm on his face. Jellicoe stood up and strolled over to pay for the coffees.

The barista turned to make the coffee. A minute later he placed to tiny espresso cups in front of Burnett. The chief inspector stared down at the tiny cups three-quarter full with the striped hazelnut crema. Then he turned to Jellicoe.

'Is that it?'

Jellicoe nodded.

'Not much is it?'

Jellicoe smiled and told him to put sugar in both. Burnet did so and then drained his cup. This seemed to act like an electric light switch for his eyes shot open.

'Take the other one,' said Jellicoe.

'You sure?'

Burnett drained this cup also. He was on the point of ordering another one when Jellicoe intervened. A Burnett with three espressos rattling around his senses was more than Rome, never mind he, was ready for.

Burnett wandered back over to the table just as two men entered the bar. Jellicoe recognised Geno Muro from the previous night. The other man was unfamiliar. Like the photographer he had thick dark hair slicked back, but this is where the comparison ended. While Geno looked permanently rumpled, the other man was taller, neatly dressed in a suit that was made to measure. He sported a well-groomed if rather thick moustache that highlighted his relative youth rather than disguising it.

'This is Silvio,' said Geno when they arrived at the table. He glanced over to the man at the bar and gave a nod. Obviously, a regular thought Jellicoe. They all shook hands and sat down. There was no small talk. Silvio went straight to business.

'Why are you here Mr Jellicoe?'

Four glasses arrived on the table and a bottle of white wine. Jellicoe groaned inwardly but Burnett's face lit up like a child looking at a birthday cake.

Jellicoe waited for the barman to serve the wine. Once he'd departed, He took the two Italians through the story of his wife's murder. Then he showed the photograph of Sylvia and Stephen in Café Doney.

'Do you know who these people are?' asked Silvio.

Jellicoe identified his father-in-law and Sylvia then he pointed to the two men that Paolo Nesta had identified. Silvio raised his eyebrows and fixed his eyes on Jellicoe.

116

'Yes and I'm sure you know who they are now,' said Silvio shrewdly.

Jellicoe smiled grimly. Then Silvio pointed to the other man. 'But not this man?' Jellicoe shook his head. Silvio studied the man closely then showed it to Geno. The little photographer shrugged.

'Do you know who he is?' asked Jellicoe.

'No. I'm sorry, just the two men Nesta knew,' replied Silvio. The he added, 'Can I have this?'

'That depends,' Jellicoe. 'How are you going to help me?'

Silvio did not answer the question directly. Instead, he began to interrogate Jellicoe about his father-in-law and the frequent trips both Sylvia and he had made to Rome and Milan. As they were speaking in Italian with occasional updates from Jellicoe, Burnett contented himself with enjoying the wine. Jellicoe quietly marvelled at his capacity to bounce back from the previous evening's epic conviviality.

Finally, Silvio appeared satisfied that he'd heard everything Jellicoe had to share. The precision of his questions suggested he was either a policeman or a journalist. Jellicoe suspected the latter given his association with Geno. Moments later he confirmed this.

'Mr Jellicoe, I run a weekly magazine called Realita!. Unlike some of the other weekly magazines we are more investigative. We do not deal in celebrity and gossip. He took out a magazine from his pocket and handed it to Jellicoe. On the cover was a beautiful Italian woman wearing a bikini. This made both Jellicoe's and Burnett's eyebrows shoot up.

Silvio shrugged but it was clear he was faintly embarrassed.

'We still have to sell magazines otherwise we go out of business. Our editorial is primarily about investigating crime and corruption in this country.'

'Can I keep this?' asked Jellicoe.

'Yes,' Silvio before a ghost of a smile appeared when he added, 'No charge.'

Jellicoe studied the man before him. His large brown eyes suggested both intelligence and cunning. They were still dancing around the topic of what Silvio wanted, although Jellicoe already knew how he could help the investigation.

'You want to have exclusive access to this story.'

'Correct.'

'Why should I give you access to this story rather than Paolo Nesta?'

Silvio's waved dismissively in the air.

'The difference between me and Nesta is that he reports; I investigate. He will write down everything the police tell him, everything the judges tell him, everything I tell him. Ask him to find who killed Wilma Montesi or your wife, he wouldn't know where to begin. He is a good man, Nesta. I like him. I think he likes me. We both want this country to be a modern, democratic country which proudly stands beside others in Europe or on the world stage, free of foreign influence, like America, but this cannot be so if we are riddled with the crime and corruption that afflicts us currently. Your story, Mr Jellicoe, the death of your wife, is the story of modern Italy. We are exporting many things now: cars, fashion, film, but also crime. In fact, crime is our greatest export. I think you must know by now that your wife's family were involved with organised crime.'

Jellicoe nodded.

'You must also know that her death was directly connected to the wars that break out between gangs. Tell me one thing, who was the other person killed by this famous "Black Cab Killer". What was their connection to your wife?'

Jellicoe had walked out of Scotland Yard almost a year ago. The official story was that he took compassionate leave before going to work on the south coast to recover from his grief. This was not true. He had been angered by the handling of the case, by the obduracy of the lead investigators who insisted on searching firstly of evidence that he was guilty then wasting time looking for a connection between Sylvia and the other woman murdered.

Shirley Kenyon, the other victim, was a waitress at a gentlemen's club in St James's. She had been killed two days before, in a black cab. No one had seen the murder take place. Neither taxi driver had seen the killer and only the young mother could swear it was a man. Months of investigation had unearthed no connection between the two women. Kenyon had been in her early forties, a divorcee with no children and a rather chequered relationship with the law. She existed at the other end of the social spectrum from Sylvia Jellicoe.

Jellicoe had no doubt that the same man had committed both murders. However, the message that had been sent to Scotland Yard following the second murder, claiming responsibility and taking up the name already coined by the press, "The Black Cab Killer" had been for Jellicoe, either a hoax or a piece of misdirection.

'There was no connection to my wife.'

'But it was the same man?'

'I believe so. Now that I know more about my wife's family, I'm certain she was the target; not Shirley Kenyon.'

'I think you are right,' said Silvio. 'Your Scotland Yard was not aware of the connection to the Mafia?'

'They're still not aware. Sylvia's mother, Claudia, gave the photograph a couple of days ago. The first I knew of it was when Paolo Nesta identified two of the men.'

'If you let me have the photograph and promise to give me first and full access to the story I will try and find out who the other man is.'

'Would Carlo Meazza know?'

'You can ask him yourself. He is a friend of mine. He took the photograph on the cover of the magazine I gave you.'

'I'd like to meet him. Can you arrange it?'

Silvio nodded then took the photograph from Jellicoe.

'Do others have this?' asked Silvio, brandishing the photograph.

'Yes,' said Jellicoe. 'When can I see him?'

'I think he is a Cinecittà tomorrow with Emilia. Perhaps you can meet him then, and the young lady. Would you like that?'

Jellicoe smiled and glanced at the young model whose face adorned so many newsstand magazine covers and advertising posters.

'That is a yes then,' said Silvio with a grin. 'Good we have a deal. I will arrange the meeting and try and find out who this man is, and you keep me informed of everything.'

'How can I reach you?' asked Jellicoe.

Silvio fished a business card from his pocket and handed it to Jellicoe. At this point the barman brought over some antipasti for the table. Silence descended on the group as they ate. When they had finished Silvio fixed his eyes on Jellicoe again.

'Tell me, have you heard of the sicari?' Jellicoe frowned his answer. His Italian vocabulary was still a little limited. 'It means hitmen,' said Silvio in English,' explained Silvio. Jellicoe wondered where the journalist was going with this.

'It seems you haven't. There are many men in the Mafia who kill. There are even some who think of themselves as sicari, but there are, we believe, a few men, an elite of no more than two or three, who the Mafia brings in for specific jobs. They kill people when a gang does not want to be directly associated with the killing. Believe it or not, most of the time they do not care who knows. Not always, however. These men kill people quickly then silently disappear again into the shadows. They are independent from the gangs and work with anyone that pays them. They have no loyalty except to money.'

'Do you think the man in the photograph is a sicaro?'

'It is possible. No one knows who they are; even the gangs have no idea, I understand. There is a conspiracy of silence surrounding them. They are your friend, and they are your enemy. They can be useful hence the reason that no one from the families has tried to stop them.'

'And the police?'

Silvio waved his hand dismissively. He said, 'They would love to catch them but because they deal at arm's length from the gangs, no one has come near to catching them.'

'Why do the gangs need to hire in assassins. I would have thought that they have any number of men capable of pulling a trigger.'

Silvio shrugged and removed a packet of cigarettes from his pocket. Jellicoe and Burnett both declined but it did give the chief an excuse to smoke his pipe. Moments later he was borrowing a match from Silvio and lighting his pipe.

'For sure they have lots of men who are killers but sometimes you want to be absolutely certain, and you want, shall we say, ambiguity. They provide both.'

'And there is more than one of these men?'

'We think so unless they have the ability to be in two places at the same time. There have been murders that have their hallmark that took place at different ends of the country. So to answer our question, yes. They may work together; they may be independent. No one knows.'

'Do you think that one of these men killed Sylvia?'

Silvio lit a cigarette and dragged slowly on it.

'The reason I am telling you this, Mr Jellicoe, is to warn you. By doing what you are doing, you are placing both yourself and Mr Burnett in great danger. To answer your question: one of the sicari has a signature way of killing his victims. It's usually in a public place. No one ever sees him. He always uses a knife. They call him "Il Cacciatore". Do you know what that means?'

Jellicoe shook his head.

'In English it means "the hunter". This man is very dangerous Mr Jellicoe. I repeat, you must tread carefully. Better still, go home now. If you are not already a target, you soon will be.'

15

Jellicoe and Burnett returned to the Grand Flora in one piece much to the chief inspector's surprise if his shouts at the Roman traffic was any guide. Any time a car came within ten feet of them he would wave his fist at them not realising that his efforts to establish a secure space around them were, in fact, destabilising the bike. A few short words of rebuke from Jellicoe managed to calm the irate older man.

It was early afternoon and the heat bouncing of the street was like a flames in a fire. Jellicoe wanted nothing more at that moment than to have another bath and change into clothes that were not wringing with sweat. The lack of sleep was beginning to tell. His mind felt as if someone was slowly applying the brakes. He felt lethargic and badly in need of a few hours' sleep before they headed out for the night.

They arrived back at the hotel to find their shadow reading the afternoon Corriere. Jellicoe saluted him on the way past. The policeman also saluted him in manner of speaking which raised a laugh from Burnett. As they went towards the lift, Jellicoe heard man calling for him. he turned around to find a receptionist waving to him. In his hand was a piece of paper. Jellicoe strolled over to the desk. The piece of paper turned out to be an envelope. He opened it up and found a telegram inside. The note was cryptic, but Jellicoe suspected he knew what it meant.

OSTIA HARBOUR 1:00AM – SHIPMENT OF ANTIQUES LEAVING ON SILK ROAD

Burnett looked at the telegram. One eyebrow raised slowly. He said, 'Is that what I think it is?'

'I have a feeling Claudia has begun to dismantle the family business and she's taking down everyone with it.'

*

It was difficult to know who was more surprised by Jellicoe's appearance at the police headquarters. The shadow Conti had assigned the two policemen or the great man himself. Conti glared at the unfortunate policeman as if it were his fault. Burnett, who shared a similar rank to Conti, enjoyed the silent theatre between the chief and his subordinate.

'I like his style,' said Burnett as he watched disinterestedly as the Commisario remonstrated with the poor man he'd detailed to keep an eye on the British policemen through hand gesture and scowl. 'You must teach me these hand gestures. I'll never pick up the language, but I think I can manage them easily enough.'

Jellicoe made a mental note not to teach the chief any such thing. They waited for Conti to finish with his subordinate before following him into his office. As they walked in, Burnett whistled appreciatively. Conti enjoyed a space that was at least three to four times larger than Burnett's office, with high ceilings and view over Rome that took in St Peter's on the horizon. He didn't much like the brown walls. It was a bit too hot for his liking also. Aside from that, he could handle

124

working in just such an environment. Best of all, he was in a place that was secluded from his direct reports. Sometimes the detectives' room felt a little bit too oppressive for his liking.

'Chief Inspector Burnett,' said Conti, extending his hand. He merely nodded to Jellicoe. Probably something to do with rank respecting rank. He waved for the two men to sit down. They quickly established that Burnett did not speak Italian and Conti's English would was rudimentary. Jellicoe acted as translator.

'May I ask why you are here?' asked Conti.

'I was probably not very forthcoming when we met earlier,' said Jellicoe. 'I apologise.'

Conti nodded but hardly seemed very mollified. Like most of the Italians Burnett had met, he seemed to be a chain smoker. Burnett took out his pipe and showed it to Conti. He received a curt nod. He ignored Jellicoe's rolling eyes. Conti waited for Jellicoe to continue.

'How much do you know of my wife's murder?'

Conti had spent much of the morning familiarising himself with the case. Much to his irritation, this had involved three men that he could ill afford to use. One to shadow the visitors, one to contact Scotland Yard to understand more about the details and one to obtain newspaper reports on the murder. Even then he had spent another half hour on the phone with his friend Paolo Nesta to find out more about what had passed between them the previous evening.

'I am acquainted with the general facts,' admitted Conti before adding brusquely. 'Why are you here?'

Jellicoe extracted one of the last remaining copies of the photograph of his wife and father-in-law. He handed it to Conti and said, 'I meant to give you this earlier, but you didn't stay long enough.'

Conti snatched the photograph from Jellicoe and studied it for a moment. He would have made a good poker player in Jellicoe's estimation for his face barely registered any emotion. He fixed his eyes on Jellicoe once more.

'Do you know who these men are?'

Jellicoe replied, 'The man at the end with his hand in front of his face is the only one I do not know.'

'Who is this?' asked Conti, pointing to Stephen Temple.

'That's my father-in-law. Nesta told me about Lentini and De Luca. Do you know the last man?'

Conti's eyes returned to the photograph. He shook his head. Then he put the photograph in his pocket.

'Did you come here just to give me this?'

'No,' replied Jellicoe. 'There's something else.' With that he handed Conti the telegram. Although it was written in English, Jellicoe suspected that the Italian would be able to understand. After a few moments, the Commisario glanced up with a frown. It was time for Jellicoe to reveal his hand.

'My mother-in-law, Claudia Temple, gave me this photograph a few days ago. Until then, I had thought that my father-in-law was an antiques dealer. He sold antique Italian and other European furniture in London. When we met Paolo Nesta and he explained to us who the men were in the photograph. Another possibility occurred to me both about what my father-in-law was really up to and why my wife was killed.'

'Why was you wife killed?'

'I can't be certain, but I now think it was connected to some sort of internecine gang warfare. My father-in-law thought I had killed Sylvia. When I was cleared at the inquest, he realised that she had been killed because of what he was.'

'Have you spoken to him about this?'

'No, he shot himself last week. I think that this telegram has come from my mother-in-law, Claudia. I think she wants revenge on the men who have robbed her of her daughter and her husband.'

'You think that this ship, the Silk Road, is going to load drugs to be carried to England?'

Jellicoe nodded. Conti silently stared into the eyes of the Englishman. A few second later he seemed satisfied. He picked up the office phone. Whoever he was calling did not answer.'

'Cristo..."

He rose angrily from his desk and stalked over to the door. Burnett, who had been contentedly puffing on his pipe, elbowed Jellicoe gently.

'Do I get on like that?' asked Burnett with faux innocence.

'Yes,' said Jellicoe sourly. This was met with a delighted chuckle.

Two men appeared in the room. One of them was the policeman Jellicoe had met earlier. The second was an older man who positively radiated seniority in the way he carried himself. His movement were slow but not ponderous. He was more ecclesiastical than judicial, but this is what Jellicoe guessed he was, a prosecuting magistrate. He had one of those faces which suggest a taste for either medieval torture, or worse, French poetry.

Prosecutors in Italy often worked closely with the police especially when it came to dealing with organised crime. The man was as tall as Jellicoe but much larger in scale. He seemed satisfied with himself and appeared to believe that others should be satisfied with him also.

In a few short sentences, Conti explained to the senior man about the two Englishmen, the telegram that had been received and its implications. The smug expression on the face of the judge changed immediately. He looked suspiciously at Jellicoe then Burnett. This was always likely to provoke a response from Burnett who had a long standing and deep-seated dislike for pomposity after years of working with Superintendent Frankie. He raised his pipe, smiled broadly and nodded. Jellicoe suspected he was irritated that he had not been introduced to the senior man. This was his revenge.

The older man and Conti spoke so rapidly to one another that Jellicoe found it difficult to follow all that was being said. As far as he could tell, the older man was questioning the credibility of the interpretation and he had a few choice phrases to describe his feelings towards Burnett that Jellicoe did pick up on and would gleefully share afterwards. This appeared to require him to shout. His eyes were in a race with a vein at the side of his head to see which would pop first. Jellicoe had the feeling he lost his temper frequently just to keep it in shape.

Conti, to his credit in Jellicoe's eyes, maintained his composure and gave every impression that he believed the two Englishmen. He was making the case to stake out the harbour at Ostia and prepare to raid the Silk Road while it's cargo was being loaded, and he was clearly winning the argument.

A few minutes later, the man left leaving Conti with the younger policeman.

'Who was that?' asked Burnett.

Conti answered in English, 'Judge Sacca,' before adding in a distinctly sour tone, 'My boss.'

Jellicoe looked sideways at Burnett who was grinning like a schoolboy with a girlie mag.

'Can we join you tonight?' asked Jellicoe. He knew it was an outside bet, but it was worth a try.

'No, Mr Jellicoe. Neither you nor the chief inspector will be anywhere near the port tonight. In fact, the only place you are going is home. I have sent a telegram to Scotland Yard to complain about your presence here. I imagine that you will be hearing from them very soon,' said Conti. There was enough controlled irritation in his voice to suggest that he wouldn't be changing his mind about them anytime soon.

Jellicoe had little doubt that they would soon hear from London. This was out of his control. He would deal with the consequences when he returned. How this would affect Burnett was more of a problem for him, but the chief seemed not to care so Jellicoe decided to let this slide. As for the Italian police, they would have their hands full setting up the raid and dealing with its aftermath. This would give Jellicoe and Burnett space and time to follow up on sicari.

It was now after three in the afternoon. Jellicoe felt as if his body and his mind was wading through gelatine. For the next few minutes Jellicoe robotically answered questions from Conti and the police sergeant who was named Panetta. They captured more details of Stephen Temple' antique business. They were also very interested in Claudia Temple. This was unsurprising as, by now, Jellicoe was somewhat curious himself to understand how much she knew of the connection between her husband and organised crime. Although he wanted to avoid making assumptions, it was difficult to avoid the conclusion that Claudia not only knew about her husband's potential criminal activities but that she, too, might be connected in some way. A part of him rebelled at the idea. This was partly because Claudia, with her delicate, cultured beauty, had always seemed a world away from the corruption and degeneracy he associated with the underworld. It was also a desire not to fall into the trap of equating any Italian with organised crime. Yet how else could he explain the telegram? She had to have known something of Stephen Temple' business. It was not a big step from this to ask if this extended to being from a crime family herself.

Just before four, Conti said that the two men could leave. Even Burnett's unusually good mood was slowing wilting in the heat of the office and the persistence of the questioning. Even the trip back to the hotel was less of a drama. By the time they returned to the hotel, the two men were happy to flop on the beds and catch up on some of the sleep they had denied themselves the previous evening.

The two men slept for a couple of hours until they were woken by the sound of the phone by Jellicoe's bed. Drowsily Jellicoe picked up the phone.

'Yes?'

'Mr Jellicoe?'

'Yes?'

'It's Silvio. I spoke with Carlo, he's happy to meet you tomorrow at Cinecittà. Maybe around four in the afternoon.'

'Who was that?' asked Burnett rubbing the sleep from his eyes.

'Silvio. We'll meet the photographer tomorrow.'

'What are we doing now?'

'I said we'd meet my American friend, Culver for cocktails at the Café de Paris.'

'I have to tell you son; this doesn't feel much like detective work. Do you actually have a plan apart from, as far as I can see, making us targets?'

Jellicoe smiled at this. The answer was 'no'. However, his presence in Italy had already started events moving. Where they were headed was anyone's guess. All they could do was focus their attention on the mystery man in the photograph, but what then? He might be involved but how to prove this? He might not be involved; in which case they had hit a dead end. Sylvia's death along with Shirley Kenyon would probably end up in a file marked 'unsolved'.

Perhaps this was to be the way. Defeat. An inglorious, comprehensive and chastening failure. Yet, considered in a different way there was something they had done to change things, to disrupt the narrative of disappointment. The raid tonight, if successful, would stem the flow of narcotics into Britain. This was something and right at that moment he needed some small victory to cling onto. Jellicoe, by now, had developed a good line in guilt. Perhaps it was the Catholic in him, but he welcomed it. The love he'd felt for Sylvia had died convincingly but a debt had been incurred. He would pay it back somehow.

16

Italy 1944

Monte Cassino, Italy: April 1944

He'd arrived late to the party. It was there on their on the faces of the young men, aged beyond their years. Worry lines flared out across mouths tightened with tension and fear. Sunken, bloodshot eyes looked on, dully and in acceptance of the inevitability of what lay ahead. Yes, he'd arrived late to a party without broads and booze and all the good things he'd enjoyed right up until the moment they had shipped him over here. To Europe. To Italy.

To the war.

Nineteen years old. All around him where old men of the same age. He tried to talk to a few of them, but their replies were monosyllabic. He later learned this was not because they were rude or, indeed, tired although they clearly were. It was because they had seen dozens if not hundreds of young men like him arrive and die. They had reached the point where to make friends was an invitation to suffer untold grief.

But that came later.

So much he would understand would come later and later would only be days away. The platoon was pressing hard against the Germans who were dug in around what was left of the monastery. For months then weeks the Americans had thrown everything they could at them, but they would not move. In fact the act of throwing so much at them had only created the conditions by which the Germans could hold on. They rubble at Monte Cassino made for an excellent cover. The Germans exploited this to the full.

Over the first few days the boy learned how to dig himself in to avoid shrapnel. He learned how to look at death and not flinch. He learned to shoot a rifle at other human beings. Slowly all of these things became easier. After a week he was almost a veteran. Almost but not quite.

The first confirmed kill, at least in his own mind, came after ten days when they attacked the outer perimeter. One German soldier left his head up too long and 'pop', he had him. If this had happened the week previously he would probably have been sick. It wasn't quite so bad as he'd thought. At least not then. Later when the dreams came it was worse. That was for the future. Then, as suddenly as they'd started, the dreams stopped. It was not so much an act of will as acquiescence to the core of a man's nature, the very soul that we do not talk about and can barely acknowledge; we are killers. Bizarrely he thought of the time he used to go to church. How his mother would insist he confess his sins. What would he say now. What would be his penance?

That he survived Monte Cassino was a surprise to him. However, getting out of Anzio with only a shaving nick was miracle. He left Monte Cassino after it finally fell in May 1944 and ended up in an even greater hell hole at the Anzio beachhead. Who's boneheaded idea was it to come here, he would often say to anyone that would listen. They weren't.

They were too busy praying as the bombs fell and the Luftwaffe strafed them into dust. They broke through and made it to Rome.

Rome.

The eternal city was everything he'd seen in the books and the films, and yet more. He was a New Yorker. He knew what cities looked like and yet when he saw Rome for the first time, the ruins, the Vatican, the piazzas and the girls, he fell in love. He did not want to leave. You can't be a tourist when you're there to fight. There was a war on. So they left and moved up towards France.

He didn't think about killing now. His only goal was surviving. Yet killing had been for him a remote exercise. It didn't feel personal. How can it be when the men you are killing are trying to kill you from behind a boulder, a bush or a building? It's just business; a ghastly business but business all the same. When the bullets whizzed past him he didn't take it personally.

They reached France. Operation Dragoon was the code name for the landing of the Allies in Provence, in southern France at the beginning of August 1944. Somewhere on the northern French coast he'd heard that his boys were bearing the brunt of the fighting. It was difficult to find more than academic interest in this. He'd done more than his fair share.

More and more now he noticed that they were taking to heart the implications of Patton's famous piece of advice: the only good German is a dead German. Time and again he would see soldiers disappear off with German prisoners. They would return. The prisoners would not. He kept his head down literally and metaphorically.

This wilful blindness could not last the war. It didn't last his teens.

The day before his twentieth birthday, they'd fought a bloody encounter with a unit of Germans left behind to slow the advance. Most of them had been wounded and would only have slowed down the retreat. Finally, after a fire fight that seemed to last the whole day, they saw the white flags appear. No one believed a white flag any more. Too many young men had died at the hands of Germans who had claimed to be surrendering. They waited for the Germans to start walking towards them, hands up.

Then the captain turned to him. There was a strange expression on his face as if he were puzzled. Then he said, 'You haven't had a turn yet, son.'

He knew what was being said. It didn't have to be spelt out. He nodded then shook his head, unsure if the answer was yes or no.

'Deal with them son.'

He nodded and took his machine gun. There were no thoughts in his head as he mowed them down. Nothing. No thoughts of Davey or Woody or Disney or dozens of other boys he'd known over the past few months. Known but not been friends with.

The German soldiers collapsed like nine pins on a bowling alley. One of the last Germans seemed confused. It was almost comical. You started it, he thought. Around him some of the newer boys looked at him. Then they didn't look young anymore. This was war; nothing more and nothing less. Morality existed no more. War had dirtied him now beyond the capacity of confession to cleanse. They were all in it together.

All the way.
Whatever it took.

⏁

17

Café de Paris, Rome: 21st August 1959

Early evening, dressed, once more, like two English actors at a country house, Jellicoe and Burnett found seats on the street outside the Café de Paris. It was just before six. The plan was to meet Culver for a few cocktails before finding a restaurant. Burnett's head moved like a spectator at Wimbledon, cheerfully enjoying his front row seat at the catwalk show of models who sashayed past him.

'A man could get used to this,' he said unabashedly.

The coughing and spluttering nearby of a scooter that was on its last wheels announced the arrival of Culver accompanied by his bulldog, Marilyn. Burnett rolled his eyes when he saw the bulldog.

'She gets lonely,' explained the American, picking her up and putting her on Burnett's lap. The two creatures looked at one another. Jellicoe had the impression neither was impressed by what they saw.

'Are you two related by any chance?' asked Culver pretending to compare Burnett and bulldog.

'You may have a point there Culver,' said Jellicoe.

Marilyn decided to lick Burnett's face as a peace offering. Even Burnett had to smile at this. 'I'm irresistible,' concluded Burnett.

'Hey listen guys,' said Culver. 'My pal Dino is working here tonight. He may know this guy you're after. What did you think of Paolo? Good guy.'

Jellicoe nodded but he suspected Burnett was less impressed by the fact that Nesta had almost certainly tipped off the police about their why they were in Rome even if it had been done with the best of intentions in mind.

'Yes, he was very helpful. He was able to identify all but one of the men,' said Jellicoe.

Culver took the Corriere out of his pocket and opened it to the page where Jellicoe and Burnett's photograph appeared.

'You made quite a splash last night. Are you planning something similar tonight?'

Jellicoe was certainly not planning to drink so much but he was not averse to more publicity. Scotland Yard would no doubt be in touch soon, so they had little enough time left to rattle the cage.

'I think a quiet night ahead. I'm going to go around some of the bars tonight and see if anyone know who the man is.'

'What if that turns up nothing?'

'We're meeting Carlo Meazza tomorrow afternoon at Cinecittà.'

Culver whistled at this news.

'I'm impressed, when are you meeting him? And how did you manage that? Carlo used to be one of the wolf pack of photographers then he discovered Emilia, now he's on the other side of the door in nightclubs and they're chasing him.'

'Silvio organised it. We'll see him at four. Is he dating this young girl?'

Culver erupted into a great belly laugh that made Marilyn flinch slightly.

'I doubt it. She's pretty safe with him if you catch my drift.'

Jellicoe did as did Burnett who said, 'Is he a bit of a p_?' He was interrupted by the arrival of a tall man dressed in a dark trousers, a white shirt with a white bow tie.

'Dino,' exclaimed Culver rising to his feet. He shook Dino's hand and turned to the two policemen. 'Hey guys, meet Dino. He's been over here, like me since forty-four. We met five years ago. I heard this jerk speak and I said to myself, that guy's from the Bronx or I'm Santa Claus.'

'Merry Christmas,' said Dino, overhearing his friend.

Jellicoe rose to his feet, but Burnett was forced to stay seated as Marilyn was now curled up on his knee having a snooze.

'Dino meet Nick and Marilyn's boyfriend over there is Reg. Guys this is Dean Little. Dino to his friends.' This made Burnett scowl, but his expression changed as a waiter set poured some white wine into his glass. Dino sat down at the table with them.

'You guys are famous now,' said Dino pointing to the photograph. His accent was similar to Culver's as far as Jellicoe could tell.

'Don't remind me,' said Jellicoe. 'I gather you work here.'

'Yes, 'I'm sorry I missed you last night – been here since it opened last year. Before that I was at Bricktop's and Strega, Doney, you name it, I've worked there. They get a lot of American tourists so there's always work for me. I gather you have some folk you want identified.'

139

Jellicoe nodded and pulled one of the remaining photographs from his pocket. He needed to make more copies. He handed it over to the American. Dino and Culver both studied the photograph while Jellicoe and Burnett studied their reaction. Dino's eyes widened slightly while Culver remained neutral. The two men did not exchange any other sign. It was obvious to the two policemen that they both recognised the two criminals with Stephen Temple. Would Dino have seen the other man? The American handed the photograph back to Jellicoe.

'I know this guy and this guy,' said Dino pointing to the two men identified by Nesta. 'Is the lady your wife?'

Jellicoe nodded to this but said nothing.

'Beautiful girl. I'm really sorry, buddy, and sorry I can't help more. Do you want me to ask some of the boys inside? Maybe they'll recognise this guy.'

Burnett answered that immediately.

'That's an idea son. Would you do that?'

'Sure,' said Dino, rising from the table. He took the photograph back from Jellicoe and headed back into the bar.

'I think you're going to need some more of those,' said Burnett indicating the photograph.

'I was thinking that, too,' said Jellicoe. 'Maybe Geno will do some for me.' He nodded in the direction of the little photographer who was standing by his scooter, smoking a cigarette just across the road. Jellicoe waved over to him. Geno jogged across the road seemingly oblivious to the oncoming traffic.

'Italians are bonkers,' observed Burnett calmly while watching Geno dodge around scooters and cars. Jellicoe handed him his last copy of the photograph and spoke rapidly to him. Then Jellicoe handed him some money. Geno nodded and promised to have more pictures the next day. Then the photographer returned by the route he'd come, once more narrowly avoiding being impaled on all manner of vehicles speeding along Via Veneto.

Dino returned ten minutes later with a man dressed in a smart suit that Jellicoe had seen the previous night. He was in his forties and smoothly handsome.

'Hey guys, this is my manager, Nicola di Nozzi. Mr di Nozzi tells me he's seen this guy before.'

Jellicoe stood up and shook hands with Di Nozzi as did Burnett. At this point Dino left them but his manager sat down at the table. He nodded to Culver and smiled. Di Nozzi spoke English. He explained that he'd worked for a time in the US in a Manhattan bar.

'I have seen this man before. He comes here from time to time. I think he is a businessman because I have not seen him in the newspapers.'

'You don't know his name.'

Di Nozzi shrugged and held his arms out. Then he added, 'It is not possible to know everyone. The regulars yes, but this man is not so often here for me to remember him, and don't forget it is August. Until Ferragosto it is little quieter for locals, but they are coming back now. Mostly it is still tourists like yourselves.'

The last remark was said with enough irony for Jellicoe to suspect that his reasons for being here were becoming very well known. Perhaps Dino had said something or maybe it was the picture from the Corriere.

'Ferragosto finished last week?' asked Jellicoe.

'Yes the fifteenth, they've been slowly returning to Rome from the coast. No one works in August, except me of course,' said Di Nozzi with a laugh.

After Di Nozzi left them they stayed a little longer before looking for a restaurant. Just before they departed. Dino came over to them once more.

'I finish around midnight. If you guys want I can take you to a few places around here and speak to some of the barmen. I know a lot of them. Maybe they might recognise this guy.'

This made sense and they agreed to return around midnight to see the American. They wandered down Via Veneto. It was night now; the pavements were crowded. So was the road. Cars and scooters battled for space on the road. The music of the night was horns rather than jazz. It was incessant. Italians used their corn horn rather than their brake. Gangs of photographers roamed the bars and rode, often two at a time, on a Vespa or Lambretta scooter that buzzed and weaved in and out of the traffic.

The two men passed outdoor tables where German and American tourists were relentlessly ripped off, yet they probably still tipped the waiters. Jellicoe found it all intoxicating. Even someone as innately ill-tempered as Burnett enjoyed the mood, the noise, the haphazardness of it all. Rome was like a dream at that moment. Like all dreams, Jellicoe knew it would end sooner or later.

Or perhaps it would herald the start of a nightmare.

*

Just after midnight, Jellicoe and Burnett returned to Café de Paris. Dino was waiting for them smoking a cigarette. As they walked down Via Veneto, Dino told them more about his life during the war and then just following it.

'When I first came to Rome I had a ball. After Anzio especially. Every day it seemed we were being hit morning, noon and night. Rome was like a celebration. The locals were happy to see us. When I say locals, I mean the girls. Man it was the best time. I didn't want to leave. I'd met a girl, Cinzia she was called. I almost walked away from the army there and then. A few did, I remember. Anyway, after Germany surrendered they asked me if I wanted to stay on. I said yes. I mean, by then I was twenty-one, twenty-two. The girls were very grateful to have us around. Then in forty-seven they said I could either sign up for another five years or go home. I thought about Italy immediately and came down.'

'What about your family in the States?' asked Jellicoe.

'My dad used to beat me up for fun. I didn't owe him anything. My mom, well she left a long time ago. Never really knew her. Italy was a better bet. I learned some of the language when I was stuck in the foxhole. I thought why not? Of course, Cinzia was married by then, but I didn't mind.'

'Are you married?'

'Engaged. We'll marry in October. She lives just off Via Tuscolana.'

They were now outside a bar called Caffe Doney which shared the same building as the Excelsior Hotel. It was probably where the photograph had been taken. This set the pattern for the next hour: Dino would have a few words with the doorman who would look at the photograph followed by a number of the waiters and barmen. They visited the nearby Caffe Strega next followed by some nightclubs, Bricktop's and the Jockey Club. None of these nightspots threw up anyone who had seen the mysterious man, so Dino led them to a street just off Via Veneto to a small jazz bar named Club 84.

'It used to be called Victor Bar. If you wanted to find drugs then you went there. Not surprisingly the cops, sorry, no disrespect, shut it down. It was pretty wild. The music was great if you liked jazz.'

'You like jazz?' asked Jellicoe. He ignored the groan from Burnett.

'Yes, I love it. I play drums sometimes with some other guys.'

'American?'

'No Italian. They like jazz here. We get some big names from time to time. Not many of the Americans but locals and the French, like Reinhardt.'

There was music playing as they went in, but it was not jazz. It sounded more Latin American. They sat down at a free table and ordered some drinks. On a tiny stage stood a young fair-haired woman. She was not classically beautiful, but her eyes were compelling and so was her voice. It was like an instrument in itself, it soared through the notes as effortlessly as a bird. Jellicoe was sure he'd heard her voice on the radio or on a juke box. The music mixed big band, with Latin and also rock n' roll.

'Who is she?' asked Jellicoe.

'Mina,' replied Dino. 'Some voice, huh?' He seemed quite proud that his adopted city could throw up such a shimmering talent.

While Jellicoe and, even, Burnett enjoyed her set, Dino went about the staff showing the photograph. Many of them clearly recognised the man from Cafe de Paris and happily chatted to him.

The dance floor had filled up with expensively clad men and women. Age was no barrier to having a good time or attracting a younger member of the opposite sex. Young men danced with older women; older men had beautiful young girls in their arms. La dolce vita indeed, thought Jellicoe.

Dino came back ten minutes later with one of the barmen. This coincided with the end of the set by Mina. She left the stage to rapturous acclaim from the audience, none more so than the chief inspector.

'She were all right,' reviewed the critic from Her Majesty's Constabulary.

They made space for the barman, who was called Francesco. Dino leaned in to make himself heard above the noise.

'Cheecho recognises the guy,' said Dino pointing to the barman. Francesco nodded enthusiastically. 'He says that the guy comes in every couple of weeks, usually the weekend usually with a different broad. He thinks he's pretty well off but doesn't throw his money around. Cheecho says he'll give you a call if he comes in again.'

Francesco nodded hopefully once more. Jellicoe guessed there was something missing. He waited for the coda. Dino fixed his eyes on Jellicoe and winked.

'You may want to provide a reminder for my pal here, Nick, if you get my meaning.'

Jellicoe did. He handed the barman some money and told him where they were staying.

'Leave a message if we are not there. Anytime day or night. Let us know,' said Jellicoe.

Francesco took the money gratefully with a promise to contact them immediately the man entered the nightclub. Furthermore he assured the Jellicoe that he would tell the other staff too. Jellicoe hoped that this lead would not bankrupt him, but it was the only one they had at that moment.

A new singer had arrived. He was good-looking in a very Latin way but his voice thin and his singing incoherent; the trumpet player, meanwhile, sounded like he had hiccups, and the drummer was obviously stoned. Perversely Jellicoe, quite like the result.

At this point Jellicoe turned to suggest to Burnett that they turn in for the night. They'd visited half a dozen night spots and done as much as they could do for the moment. Burnett wasn't there. Jellicoe assumed he'd disappeared to the men's room until his eyes fixed on the small dance floor in front of the stage. Several men and women were dancing. One of the men was Burnett. His partner was an attractive lady with suspiciously jet-black hair. If Jellicoe were surprised that Burnett was on the dance floor it was as nothing to his amazement that the chief could actually dance. Rather well too. No one seeing Burnett for the first time would have mistaken him for Fred Astaire which made it all the more of a shock that he knew how to move. Jellicoe wouldn't have known a polka from a pair of pliers, but he did know when someone had grace or rhythm.

When the dance finished the band switched to rock n' roll and a jive. Much to Jellicoe's disappointment, the opportunity to enjoy the chief jiving was denied to him as both he and his dance partner broke out into laughter and shook their heads. They went to the table where Jellicoe was sitting, and promptly ignored him.

This left Jellicoe on his own as Dino had long since left. Just when Jellicoe was about to leave, the woman excused herself for a moment to visit the ladies room. When she was safely out of sight Burnett turned around to Jellicoe. He said in an entirely unnecessary stage whisper, 'I need some money.'

Jellicoe looked appalled. It was one thing to be sympathetic to Burnett over the problems he was experiencing in his marriage, it was quite another to fund a night with a prostitute. Burnett must have read his mind because his face turned onto a scowl.

'She's not on the game. She's a widow,' he snapped. Jellicoe still looked sceptical. This made Burnett even more surly. 'I'm not eighteen y'know.'

Yet here he was needing money. Jellicoe smiled and handed over some cash.

'Do you think she likes me?' asked Burnett.

'I think she'd rather French kiss an Alpaca,' replied Jellicoe unkindly. Conscious that he was being a little mean-spirited, he added, 'Be careful.' Afterwards as he walked home in the still warm night air of Rome, he wondered if his grin bordered on lascivious or perhaps the parental wag of the finger had tipped Burnett's language into a colourful and anatomically challenging suggestion as to what he could do with the money. He supposed his laughing all the way through the rant hadn't helped matters either. It ended just when Burnett spotted his dance partner returning from her visit to the powder room.

He took the money anyway, with a growl.

*

At around the same time that Jellicoe was making his way back to the hotel on rather steadier feet than the previous night, Commisario Fausto Conti along with twenty officers from the Polizia descended on the port at Ostia where the Silk Road had docked an hour previously. The cargo would be loaded and then the ship would depart for Britain. The policemen calmly watched as the ship's cargo was loaded then they struck. Then they swarmed first around the dockworkers and then onto the ship.

Such was the total surprise of the raid, not a single shot was fired. Conti noted this with a profound relief. Yet he knew a long night lay ahead. However, he felt confident that they would yield a result that would send tremors through organised crime from Rome through the French Connection and all the way to Indochina and beyond.

By five in the morning they had found what they were looking for. An exhausted but happy Conti celebrated with the other policemen. There seemed little point in returning home now. He fell asleep in his car an woke up a couple of hours later at eight, He went straight to the office.

18

Rome: 22nd August 1959

It was six in the morning. Rome was quiet aside from the warbling of thousands of starlings. He loved to listen to their chatter of the birds, their conversations, more than he loved Mozart and he adored Mozart. This was the Rome he loved before it was invaded by mediocre middle managers, slothful shopkeepers and vacationing visitors to the city he had adopted as his own.

He passed a kiosk that had just opened. An old woman was putting out a rack of magazines. Bikini clad women adorned some of them, others had film stars while, yet another batch had knitting patterns. The woman looked at him and nodded. He picked up Il Tempo, a local Rome newspaper and threw a few coins on the counter.

A scooter passed him by. A young man and a young woman were riding on it. Probably on their way back to her place after a night out. There were not many cars on the road yet. He crossed the road and ducked down an alley. Soon he was outside a large brown door. He inserted his keys and headed up the stairs.

Inside his apartment, he put the moka on and made himself a coffee. It took a few minutes and then he heard the gurgling and switched off the gas stove. He poured the black liquid slowly into the tiny cup. Then he took the folded newspaper and scanned the front page. Methodically, he made his way through it front to back as always.

He returned to the classified section. His eyes fixed on one particular ad in the bottom right. This was normally where he asked his clients to place them. The ads appeared only occasionally but he still had to look every day.

The ad read: Eppur si muove (and so it goes). This was followed by a telephone number and another cryptic remark which he was able to interpret as a time to call. He still had half an hour.

He ran the bath. Even a sicaro, a hitmen need to wash.

The time went quickly. Before long it was time to call the number. He rang. It was engaged. This made him swear out loud. He tried again. It was still busy. He almost slammed the phone down, but he reasoned that it was not the telephone's fault that his client's only option for contacting him was through classified ads.

Third time was no luckier, but his fourth attempt was successful.

'It's Galileo,' he said.

'This is the Pope,' came the reply.

'You were wrong about the earth.'

'I was wrong about most things,' rasped the voice in reply but it had relaxed now. There was humour and relief in the nervous laugh. Relief because this was the person they wanted to speak to, not someone curious about the cryptic message in the newspaper.

'Go on,' said the man going straight to business. This silenced the laughter at the other end of the phone.

'Read yesterday afternoon's Corriere; Victor Ciuffa page. There's an English policeman in Rome looking into the murder of Sylvia Temple.'

'Yes, I know,' said the man, a frown appearing on his forehead.

'Stop him.'

They talked for another few minutes as more details were communicated. Then the man gently put the phone receiver down. He put his elbows on the table and pressed the tips of his fingers together in a steeple.

Stop him.

In the world in which he worked trust did not exist and suspicion was survival, the words of his client were pregnant with meaning.

Stop him, but he'd worked that out already. This was a problem which threatened to spiral out of control unless he did something.

Stop him.

*

Elsewhere in Rome, the person who was the subject of this conversation was waking up from a deep sleep. He'd had the benefit of many more hours rest when awoke well refreshed to discover Chief Inspector Burnett's bed empty. His first reaction was all too male. He smiled. The smile faded quickly but for reasons less to do with any puritanical disapproval than the very real possibility that Burnett might be in trouble.

Now that his mind was a little clearer than when he'd so happily seeded Burnett's amorous adventure, he wondered how exactly the two lovebirds would be communicating. Dance and love, of course, transcend communication, they are expressions of feeling. However, unless the lady in question spoke some English, then Burnett was on a sticky wicket when the dance, so to speak, ended.

He opened the curtains to the room allowing light to flood in. Then he walked to the bathroom and began to run the bath. Just then he heard the phone ringing. His heart began to race. If something happened to Burnett he would never forgive himself. He raced out of the bathroom and picked up the phone. An Italian voice said, 'Just a moment.'

The phone clicked and then a familiar voice came on the line. 'Mr Jellicoe,' said Commisario Conti, introducing himself. 'I had a very busy night last night following your tip off.'

Jellicoe held his breath unsure if this were to do with the tip off or it was news about his chief inspector. For some reason he had never doubts the truthfulness of the information. Yet now, confronted by the man charged with executing the raid it occurred to him that perhaps this trust was premature.

'We arrested sixteen men last night and have impounded over twenty kilograms of heroin that would have been shipped to your country. The drugs originally came from Indochina via Marseilles. We will work with our sixteen suspects to find out more about the operation.'

I'll bet you will, thought Jellicoe.

'That's good news. You see what comes from Anglo-Italian cooperation,' pointed out Jellicoe.

Conti had the good grace to laugh at this, 'Indeed but I still think you should consider what I said to you yesterday. Nothing good can come of this vigilante exercise. You are putting your own life and Chief Inspector Burnett's life at risk.'

'I'm on holiday, Commisario.'

'And yet you spoke to many barmen last night about the group in the photograph you gave me.'

'I think you took it from, Commisario, but I won't quibble over the details. Thankfully, I had another one.'

'Go home, Mr Jellicoe. I mean it. You are in danger. Oh, and thank you.'

Conti rang off leaving Jellicoe with a grin on his face. It lasted a matter of seconds. The door to the room flew open and in walked Burnett.

'Bloody hell that was some night. Ah thanks for the running the bath for me. I smell like a badger's arse.'

The bathroom door shut forcing Jellicoe to spend the next fifteen minutes listening to Burnett's repertoire of Sinatra. Sometimes life was unfair, but this was Mother Nature at her most capricious.

Over breakfast Burnett steadfastly refused to say anything about the previous night but his beaming countenance was its own story. Jellicoe contented himself with the occasional shake of the head while trying to ignore the smile on his chief's face and the occasional cackle. At one point he glanced towards the distant dome of St Peter's and said, 'Do you think we can visit the Vatican?'

'Why? Do you want the Pope to dissolve your marriage or listen to your confession? Better still, maybe you and your lady friend can tie the knot there.'

Burnett was in too much of a good humour to care about his subordinate's insubordination.

'You're just jealous, son. An old man like me and I can still pull.'

'I don't want to know,' replied Jellicoe.

'First international cap,' continued Burnett, as he spread butter on a croissant. 'Anyway, good news about the drugs bust. Was Conti any happier?'

'Marginally. Still wants us out of the country.'

'I'm surprised. We're only here a day and we're already clearing up crime in the country. Imagine what it'll be like if we stay a week.'

'He didn't quite see things that way, sadly,' reported Jellicoe.

'When do we see your photographer fella?'

'Four at the film studio, Cinecittà. Who knows, chief, they may want your ugly mug in a film.'

'Why not? You said they made real films here.'

'Neo-realisme,' replied Jellicoe before adding drily, 'Not horror.'

*

The palazzo of Geno Muro was situated near Piazza Navona. Burnett's mood was upbeat following his amorous adventures of the previous evening or, perhaps, he was becoming more accustomed to dicing with death on the back of the Vespa scooter. Either way, they arrived at the piazza which was disguised behind a number of baroque buildings. Piazza Navona was one of Jellicoe's favourite places in Rome. He and Claudia had married at the Borromeo church in the piazza, Sant' Agnese in Agone.

'Bloody hell,' exclaimed Burnett. 'Is that a fountain?'

The Fountain of the Four Rivers was part fountain, part enormous sculpture located in the centre of the long rectangular Navona square. In its centre was a tall, slender, white obelisk in the Egyptian style, which had an enormous base comprising four corners, each featuring astonishing sculptures of heroic gods and animals. These symbolised the four rivers: the Nile, the Ganges, the Danube and the River de la Plata.

'The where?' asked Burnett as they walked towards the fountain.

'No idea,' admitted Jellicoe. 'I've heard of the other ones.'

'Big deal,' said Burnett sympathetically. 'So this is where you were married?'

They were standing outside Sant' Agnese in Agone. Jellicoe pointed to one of the sculptures in the fountain. It was a powerful man holding his hand up as if directly shielding his eyes from the church.

'The story goes that Bernini and the man that designed the church, Borromini were great rivals. That god is shielding his eyes from the awful sight of Borromini's church. I read also that Borromini carved a pair of donkey's ears on one of the walls of the building. Bernini lived right next to the palace, so got his own back by having a phallus sculpted on the side of his house, directed towards Borromini.'

'Bloody artists,' said Burnett unimpressed. 'Do you want to inside?' He was pointing at the church.

Jellicoe shook his head but then changed his mind. The two men trooped up the steps into the church. It all came back to him. Walking up the aisle with Sylvia. Everyone smiling on either side of them. He'd glanced up, as if to say thanks to the heavens. Instead he'd seen the frescoes inside the enormous cupola depicting the apotheosis of St Agnes. He'd done so again with Burnett.

'You were married here?' said Burnett in amazement. He shook his head in quiet disbelief.

'Let's find Geno. Too many memories here.'

They walked to the side of the church where there was a narrow alleyway that led to a street with high buildings either side.

'He lives in one of these,' said Jellicoe.

They found the address then read through the list of names of people who occupied the building. Geno lived on the top floor if Jellicoe's guess was correct. He rang the buzzer.

'Si?' came the response on his third attempt at ringing.

'Sono Nick Jellicoe.'

The door was buzzed open, and they climbed a wide, winding staircase to the top floor. Paint was peeling off the walls but notwithstanding its appearance, it appeared clean with no suspicious odours that inhabited stairwells back home.

The nameplate outside the door confirmed that this was the residence of Eugenio Muro. The door was opened so the two men took this as an invitation to enter. Geno was sitting at a dining table which dominated the small living room area. This was typical of Italian homes from what Jellicoe had seen. The house was tidy, but the table was full of empty, unwashed plates and an ashtray that had not been cleaned this year. A cigarette was glued to Geno's bottom lip.

'Welcome to my humble abode,' said Geno drily. 'Coffee?'

Jellicoe said yes so the little Italian went into the kitchen to put a large moka on his gas stove. A small kitten appeared from the bedroom. It was crown, black and white. Burnett bent down and picked it up. It began to purr.

'Cats like me,' he said in answer to a question that Jellicoe had not asked.

'Have you met Livia?' shouted Geno from the kitchen.

'Yes,' replied Jellicoe, who had joined Burnett in stroking the kitten.

The two men sat down with Livia the cat electing to sit on Burnett's knee. Geno came in with the coffees. There were three espresso cups. Geno offered sugar and then seconds later all three drinks had been consumed which left Burnett wondering why Italians bothered with the whole palaver of making such a small quantity. He had, however, begun to acquire a taste for the Italian coffee which made it all the more frustrating that he could not have more.

When they'd finished, Geno reached onto the table and removed an envelope from underneath a plate. He handed it to Jellicoe.

'Thanks for doing so quickly.'

The Italian waved this away.

'I had to develop the photographs from last night anyway. Now, I go to bed,' said the photographer. Jellicoe glanced down at the number of espresso cups on the table that could only have been consumed, he hoped, that morning. This made Geno smile. 'I can drink any amount of espresso and still sleep well.'

The two policemen left the apartment having obtained the pictures leaving Geno on his own with Livia. He sloped over to his telephone and dialled a number. It took a minute before it was answered, then spoke to the person on the other end of the line.

'They have the additional photographs now. They're going to see Carlo later. Maybe he knows who the other man is. A bit of a long shot if you ask me.'

They made their way back to where Jellicoe had parked the Vespa. Burnett sighed audibly which made Jellicoe chuckle.

'Let's have something to eat,' said Burnett. 'I'm starving.'

*

157

He was on the phone now. So much to do today. He regretted agreeing to attend the wrap party. He was saying this. Repeatedly. Then he heard a knock at the door. 'Someone's at the door. I'll have to go. See you later.'

He padded over to the door and opened it without doing what he usually did and checking who was outside through the keyhole. Standing in the corridor was a man wearing a dark suit and sunglasses.

'You? What are you doing here?'.

The man took out a knife. He stared transfixed at the steel glinting in the light of the corridor. The man's movement was adroit, as minimal as Rothko and just as anonymous. Like a hunter.

'No,' appealed the man.

It was the last thing he ever said.

19

London: Saturday 22nd August 1959

Joe Sanders gazed up at the cloudless blue sky but more in impatience than wonder. All around, men stream passed him. Some bumped into him. What might have provoked a fight in a bar was ignored here. They were brothers after all. Everyone was here for the same reason, and they were here in their thousands. Tens of thousands in fact.

The queue for the chip van shuffled forward. Ten minutes later he had what he'd been queuing up for. A bag of soggy chips. It was exquisite. What more could a man want on a day like this? Eating chips with his brothers in arms at the start of a new season. There was so much to look forward to.

He looked around him and saw men walking to the match with their sons. Sons walking with fathers and grandfathers. Three generations of fans. Together. It felt like a sucker punch. He wanted this too: to bring his son to the place of worship. There was a tap on his shoulder. He turned around and grinned at Barry Cooper.

'About time too Gary, mate.'

'Whaddaya mean about time? The match isn't for another hour and a half.'

'We can have a quick one.'

Someone began singing a song. It was quickly taken up by the crowd around the two men joined in enthusiastically.

'I'm forever blowing bubbles,' they sang, 'pretty bubbles in the air. They fly so high, nearly reach the sky.'

Nearby a group of men wearing blue and white Leicester City scarves and hats joined in but with different lyrics.

'Then like West Ham, they fade and die.'

Sanders spun around roaring abuse at the opposition supporters. His friend was appalled and so were a number of his fellow West Ham supporters.

'Leave it out, Joe.'

'Hey mate,' shouted another, 'less of the bad language. There's kids around.'

Sanders was immediately remorseful. He held his hand up and apologised before turning to Cooper.

'Bloody liberty them lot singing that.'

'Still, Joe. Kids n'that.'

'I know, I know. Speaking of which Gary, any word on my boy?'

'A mate of mine knows and ex-copper. He says he might be able to find out where the boy is.'

Sanders stopped in his tracks and smiled a mirthless grin.

'An ex-cop who might,' he said emphasising the word. 'How much does he want? If he's an ex-cop then there'll be money involved.'

'Twenty quid. Ten for him and ten for his mate on the force who'll do the checking.'

Sanders wasn't happy about this, but the last few days had thrown up nothing. Where was he going to find twenty quid and all the rest. Once those boys knew that he was prepared to

160

pay then they would feed him scraps in order to get more from him. He was in no position to bargain, though. They had him over a barrel and no mistake. As he thought about how to handle this development, he saw a pair of boys in the claret and blue walking with their dad to the stadium. Neither was older than ten. He wanted to do this with his boy. Only one thing was preventing this. He thought of Suze. It made his mouth curl, almost involuntarily, into a snarl. He wouldn't let her win. He would see his boy. He would go with his dad to Upton Park. They would cheer on 'the Hammers' together.

'Tell them that they'll get half for the information and the rest when I see my son.'

Cooper looked doubtful but he nodded. He said, 'I'll let 'im know but he won't be happy.'

The two men re-joined the throng pushing forward towards the gates. The song was restarted again. Sanders and Cooper joined full throated.

'Fortune's always hiding, I've looked everywhere, I'm forever blowing bubbles, Pretty bubbles in the air.'

20

Rome: 22nd August 1959

Just two hours before Jellicoe was due to see Carlo Meazza, he was arrested by Commisario Conti. The arrest took him by surprise but nowhere near as much as his short-lived kidnapping by Giovanni Lentini. All in all, it was a busy afternoon for Jellicoe.

As they left Geno Muro's palazzo they descended the stairs, passing a man wearing a hat and sunglasses who was on the way up. When they reached the street, Burnett complained, which was not of itself unusual. However, given his efforts of the night before, Jellicoe conceded he probably had earned an early lunch. They walked along Via della Pace and settled on a restaurant with outdoor tables adorned by red and white checked table cloths.

Along the street, Jellicoe noticed their shadow. He waved to him and invited the policeman to join them. The policeman looked away and walked over to a nearby bar. Jellicoe and Burnett both selected Pasta alla Gricia, which is a carbonara but without the eggs. They accompanied this with a bottle of Chianti.

All was going well until Burnett spilled the glass onto his powder blue Brioni suit. For the next few minutes Burnett turned the air blue with a passionate condemnation of anything and everything of which he could think. Given the duration of his rant, this was clearly quite a number of things. As the rage passed he was left with a red stain around the area of his crotch.

'Will they be able to clean this?' he asked in a voice that was perilously close to a whine.

'I'm sure they have dry cleaners who are experts in just such emergencies. It means you'll have to wear your dinner suit to the interview later. We'll go straight from here to the dry cleaners and get your dinner suit and mine.'

When they finished their meal Jellicoe paid up which, at least, had the beneficial effect of restoring some of Burnett's good humour.

'You're a kept man, chief.'

'Enjoying every second of it. You do think they can fix this suit?'

'Yes, I'm sure.'

They walked back towards Piazza Navona and hopped on the Vespa. Fifty metres ahead of them, their shadow did likewise. Just as they started their scooter, police sirens could be heard. The two scooters departed from the street at a speed designed to induce terror in Burnett.

Ten minutes later they were back at the hotel. They separated at this point. Burnett went to pick up the dinner suits and shirts they'd left in to be cleaned while Jellicoe returned to the hotel room to rest. At least that was the plan, but as von Moltke once said, no plan survives contact with the enemy.

A man stepped in front of Jellicoe as he was about to enter the hotel.

'Mr Jellicoe?'

He was tall, dressed in a dark suit with shiny black hair and sunglasses. If you wanted to attend a fancy dress party dressed as mafioso, this would probably be your costume. At least, this was Jellicoe's view. It was confirmed a moment later when the man casually revealed two things. Firstly, that he was carrying a gun. Nothing in the man's face suggested he was anything less than competent in its use. The second revelation was that he was not alone. On the other side of Jellicoe was a bald neckless man wearing a strong cologne. If bull-semen had a smell then this was probably it.

Jellicoe risked a glance towards his shadow who had elected to follow him. The man shrugged. Police surveillance was clearly a one-way street in this town. With one man either side of him, they walked towards a waiting car. None too gently, he was put in the back seat. Neither man entered the car.

Another was sitting there, smoking a cigarette. He turned to look at Jellicoe. It was a face he knew all too well. He'd seen it in the photograph of his wife. Giovanni Lentini was a businessman with shady connections to the Mafia, according to Paolo Nesta: a money launderer.

'I gather you have been asking questions about me,' he said in accented English.

This probably wasn't the time to compliment his English but, oddly, despite the danger and his discomfort on the back seat, this was the first thought that flashed through Jellicoe's head.

'Yes,' replied Jellicoe, electing to speak Italian. 'I'm trying to find out if you killed my wife or arranged it.'

The man had not looked at Jellicoe up to this point; electing, instead, to smoke his cigarette and stare out of the window in an attempt to unnerve Jellicoe with an air of I-could-have-you-killed-now-Mr-Jellicoe. To give him his due, it was working. When he heard Jellicoe say this, his head shot around and stared at the policeman. A smile crossed his face rather like that of a large snake encountering a rodent looking the wrong way.

'I did not kill your wife Mr Jellicoe. I would also add that I am sorry for your loss, but I doubt you would believe me. She was a beautiful woman. I liked her.'

'Did Matteo de Luca kill her?'

'Ahh,' replied Lentini in a voice that could have been used on a Bisto ad. 'Now we come to the reason for my visit. You have upset a number of people who I consider friends. First with your questions and then with an incident that took place last night.'

Jellicoe failed to suppress a smile but, at least managed to stop himself punching the air and shouting, 'Yes.'

'What happened?'

'Don't waste my time, Jellicoe,' snapped Lentini. 'Do you think I don't know that you fed Conti the details of the raid last night.'

'If your sources within the police are so good then why didn't you warn your friends?'

This was a pertinent question and even Lentini acknowledged this with his smile.

'We need to improve our sources within the department, clearly. Look Jellicoe, I say this as someone who liked your wife.'

'How much did you like her?'

The smile faded from Lentini's face, 'If someone chooses to stray, who do you blame, Jellicoe? I know who I would, but no matter. I repeat, as someone who liked your wife and your father-in-law, I think you need to leave Rome soon. I won't warn you again because the next time you will probably be dead.'

Lentini looked away which was clearly a signal for moments later, the powerful hands of the man who had misplaced his neck yanked Jellicoe from the back of the car and back onto the street. Jellicoe was aware that his prone position was somewhat undignified. He rose to his feet and looked down at Lentini's man. He said one word to him.

'Mooo'

Then he turned away from a man who was now dementedly angry and being restrained by the other. Jellicoe passed the detective shadow and said, 'Thanks for your help.' The detective smiled and saluted him ironically but said nothing.

Jellicoe went up to his room and lay on the bed. His heart was racing only marginally faster than his mind. There was no question now: both he and Burnett had unleashed something that would make Pandora's box seem like a child's jewellery chest.

Five minutes later he heard the banging on the door. Expecting it to be Burnett he responded a little bit more forthrightly than is customary for a detective inspector when addressing his commanding officer. The banging continued however with what sounded like Italian voices. Confused, Jellicoe opened the door to find a very flushed Commisario Conti with a number of uniformed men. Having done this himself countless times, Jellicoe viewed this as a distinctly unpromising scenario.

'Will you come with us, please?'

Jellicoe did as he was asked. Or perhaps he was getting used to being abducted by the locals. The room was immediately invaded by a couple of the uniformed men. This was more concerning. What exactly was going on?

'There's no one else,' shouted one of the officers.

'Where is Chief Inspector Burnett?' asked Conti. He didn't look as if he was in a mood to be messed around. To be fair, he never did.

Jellicoe shrugged before replying, 'He went for a walk. He didn't say where he was going.'

Conti's reddening face and scowl suggested that he did not believe this but decided not to accuse Jellicoe outright of lying. Instead, he decided quickly that he would take him away and leave a couple of men to deal with the chief inspector when he returned. They hurried down the stairs and through the lobby. Jellicoe was not cuffed but no one looking on would have been in doubt that he was arrested. The clue was the presence of two rather burly Polizia either side of him, clinging to his arms.

Burnett was certainly under no illusions when he was walking on the other side of the street from the Grand Flora, and he saw Jellicoe being bundled none too gently into a police car. He stopped immediately ten ducked behind a lamp post.

A side note for anyone who is on the run from the police. A lamp post is insufficient cover at the best of times due principally to its rather slender design. In Burnett's case, it was an even less promising avenue for evasion as he would have been the first to admit. In addition, his conspicuousness was unquestionably enhanced by the impeccably dry-cleaned dinner he suit he was wearing, minus the bow tie. It was simply too hot.

167

Realising that the lamp post was not providing the degree of concealment that his situation demanded, Burnett ducked behind a Fiat 500. The Lilliputian car was a modest upgrade on the lamp post. He watched as Conti appeared to be directing the remaining policemen. He had little doubt as to what was being said. They were clearly staying behind to keep an eye out for him.

This was a problem. A rather large one, in fact. There was little point worrying about why Jellicoe had been arrested, for that was surely what he was seeing. Thanks to Jellicoe's largesse, he had a bit of money left.

The inadequacy of his hiding place, the tiny Fiat, was soon laid bare as one of the Italian policemen spotted him across the road and shouted, 'Commisario, guarda.'

All eyes followed the line of the policeman's outstretched arm directly towards Burnett, including Jellicoe's. Burnett was no rabbit in the headlights. He moved immediately away from the Fiat towards a stationary taxi and jumped in.

21

While Jellicoe was certainly no local to Rome he knew his way around. So it came as something of a surprise to him to find the police car traveling at speed towards his intended destination at Cinecittà. They diverted off Via Tuscolana to an area he was unfamiliar with.

'What is going on, Commisario?'

'Don't you know?'

Jellicoe rolled his eyes and said nothing more for the rest of the journey. They pulled up outside a beautiful palazzo. Conti was out of the car in an instant quickly followed by Jellicoe. There were two police cars outside with a number of policemen melting in the Rome heat. The older detective bounded up the stairs like a mountain goat with Jellicoe struggling to keep up.

Outside the apartment was a policeman trying to fend off the questions of an old woman. Conti passed through without acknowledging the woman who shouted at him.

Jellicoe followed Conti into the apartment. Or at least he would have, except there was a dead body on the floor blocking his way. On the wall was a large picture of the model Jellicoe had seen many times while in Rome. He guessed that Carlo Meazza had taken his last photograph. Conti glared at Jellicoe.

'You were the last person to see him alive.'

'Correction. The murderer was the last person to see him alive, Commisario, and I have never met him. My appointment with him was for four at Cinecittà,' replied Jellicoe curtly. He was in no mood for games. Rather he felt an immense sadness, responsibility even. Had he contributed to the photographer's death. There seemed only one answer to this, and he felt wretched. Conti was detective enough to see the change on Jellicoe's face, the evident desolation. He was human enough to understand its source.

'What can you tell me?' asked Conti. His tone had changed. The game playing was at an end. He needed information now and quickly.

Jellicoe told him everything.

Conti listened in silence. Both men knew that Meazza's death was connected to the investigation that Jellicoe was pursuing. There was little point in condemning the English detective. By the look on his face the young man was going to make a good job of that himself.

When Jellicoe had finished Conti was silent then he asked, 'Where is your friend going?'

This was a good question. Burnett was not going to get very far on the money he had nor his linguistic skills in Italian which did not extend far beyond ordering a coffee or saying thank you. Perhaps his nocturnal adventures may have furnished him with some new words but none of them were likely to pass muster outside of a brothel.

'Well, I mentioned we have an appointment at Cinecittà at four with this man. Maybe he'll try and keep that.' Conti frowned. 'He took the photograph of my wife and the others. We were going to ask him about the other man in the

170

photograph.' A ghost of a smile appeared on the lips of the Italian, but he said nothing.

A noise from another room distracted the two men. Jellicoe turned and saw a couple of policeman standing amongst debris.

'What happened in there?' asked Jellicoe.

'It's a storeroom for equipment,' replied Conti.

Jellicoe walked towards it, 'Do you mind if I look?' he asked without waiting for permission.

'Help yourself,' replied Conti sarcastically.

Jellicoe went into the room. It was long and quite thin. At one end was a table with cameras laid out and lighting equipment. To the right was a floor to ceiling mahogany filing cabinet. On the front of the drawers was a brass name plate. There were dates written on the cards. Jellicoe looked along the rank of dates. Several of them had been opened and the contents removed. He went to an unopened one.

Taking a handkerchief out of his pocket, Jellicoe pulled open the drawer causing one of policemen to notice him for the first time. The policeman erupted in anger. Then he saw Conti standing at the door. Conti shook his head which quietened his more volatile colleague.

'What are you looking for?' asked Conti

The inside of the drawer contained photographs stacked neatly and negatives held with a labelled envelope. The label on the front showed the date. Jellicoe seemed satisfied by what he'd seen and replaced the drawer. His eyes quickly scanned along the dates of the drawers until he reached the date that the photograph that had been taken with Sylvia, her father with De Luca and Lentini.

This drawer was empty.

Jellicoe turned to Conti, 'He's after the photographs.'

Conti frowned, 'I had noticed.'

'No, I mean the ones where he thinks that either he appears in them or the people who are paying him. Or both. Don't you see? Because of my asking these questions, they know there are photographs taken by these swarms of photographers that may provide links between my father-in-law and organised crime.'

'They won't care,' said Conti. 'Circumstantial.'

'True, but what if there is also a photograph of this hitman with the gang leaders. We might be able to identify who it is.'

Conti thought for a moment, 'I see that but how would we know? I mean, these men, these sicaro, are leading normal lives, we think. They have made no imprint. They are shadows. How would we know who in the crowd is a hitman and who is a waiter? There will be hundreds of people to interview and cross check. We don't have the manpower for this.'

Jellicoe's mind was racing.

'He's taken only certain dates. Look. He's left most of the drawers alone. Do you have a list of the dates that he's taken?'

Conti glanced towards one of the policemen. The man nodded and handed Conti a piece of paper with handwriting on it showing the dates that had been removed. Conti showed it to Jellicoe.

There were eight dates in all including the one on the back of Jellicoe's photograph. Jellicoe stared at the photographs for a few moments then it hit him.

'Of course,' exclaimed Jellicoe. 'I'm an idiot. Why didn't I think of that?'

'What do you mean?' asked Conti?

'He knows that Meazza was in the bar that night and that he would have taken a photograph of him with one of these men,

172

possibly, but there were other photographers around that night, too. There must be at least ten of them outside the bars at one time or another. Maybe one of them was inside too.'

Conti's eyes widened slightly. He nodded at this then he turned to Panetta and said quickly, 'We need to get men to all of the photographers.'

Panetta frowned at this, but Jellicoe explained, 'They might be in danger. You're right, Commisario. Look, why don't we go to Geno Muro? Perhaps he may have something that can help us identify this man. It's still only two forty-five. The chief won't know that Meazza is dead. He'll still go Cinecittà to make the meeting. We have time to go to Muro and then to Cinecittà.'

Conti turned to Panetta, 'Get hold of Geno Muro. Find out where he lives or where he stores his photographs and tell him we are going to meet him there. Get a police car to his home immediately.' Then Conti turned to Jellicoe. He said, 'Very well Mr Jellicoe. I hope you're right.'

So did Jellicoe. Burnett was potentially in great danger now.

*

A series of ignored phone calls established that Geno Muro was a heavy sleeper. It wasn't until policemen gained entry to his palazzo and banged on the door that he was roused from his slumber and answered the door with all of the enthusiasm of a prisoner at Christmas. The news of Meazza's death sobered him immediately as did a phone conversation with Commisario Conti who suggested that he might be a target also. At this point the presence of two burly policemen became less of a burden.

Fifteen minutes later, Jellicoe and Conti arrived. Roman traffic simply melted away under the persuasive percussive

173

impact of a police siren and yet another Italian who had missed his calling as a racing driver. To give Panetta his due, he knew how to handle a car and he certainly tested its cornering ability to the fullest. DS Wallace would have been proud.

Muro greeted the arrival of Jellicoe and the two Italian policemen with a hand gesture that is immediately familiar to that demonstrative race. He pressed his right thumb against his four fingers and shook it a little. Conti answered the question posed by Muro's what-do-you-want gesture.

'We need to see your photographs from December nineteen fifty-seven. Where do you keep them?'

Like Meazza, the little photographer, notwithstanding his scruffy appearance, was actually quite organised. He informed them that they were kept at his studio which was a few minutes' walk from the apartment.

'Let's go,' said Conti, anticipating Jellicoe's own desire to move quickly.

'Can I take a shower?' asked Muro

'No,' said Conti.

This was met with a sigh. 'At least let me get dressed,' said Conti. He was wearing his pyjamas which for Muro consisted of a Lazio football shirt and shorts.

'No,' replied Conti, who supported their city rivals, Roma. This gave the Commisario some minor satisfaction as he and other Roma supporters regarded their near neighbours as 'the fascist team'.

'Can I, at least, wear shoes?' asked Muro, sarcastically.

It was tempting but Conti relented on the shoe point and soon they were rushing down the stairs and out the front door of the palazzo with Muro grumbling every step of the way. They walked for five minutes away from Piazza Navona, towards the River Tiber. Muro's studio was on the second floor above a Tabbacheria.

'Can I buy some cigarettes?' asked Muro as they reached the studio. 'I left mine back at the apartment.'

'No,' said Conti.

Muro's studio consisted of three rooms. He shared it with two other photographers who formed part of the swarm that pestered the rich and famous along Via Veneto. The first room they encountered was clearly used for taking photographs of models. There was lighting equipment neatly stacked on one corner and a single sofa in the middle. The room was painted a bright white. A second room was set aside for developing photographs according to Muro but, sensing the urgency with the three policemen, he decided against showing them. He led them into a third room where there were three cupboards. Muro marched to the furthest one and used his keys to open it up.

Inside it there were several boxes about the size of a shoe box. He removed the ones specified by Conti and placed them on a table. His filing was relatively efficient but not quite at the level of the murdered Meazza. He handed a box to each of the detectives and informed them that each covered a month of photographs but there was no order aside from this.

The policemen looked at one another. There was no choice but to start looking, but what were they looking for?

'Any photographs with De Luca and Lentini set aside,' suggested Jellicoe. This was obvious and Conti's sharp look at Jellicoe reminded him that he was not dealing with a fool. Then Jellicoe added, 'If you see any other person in the photographs that you recognise, let me know.'

For the next fifteen minutes they sifted through the photographs of Muro. They each set aside a two dozen or more pictures with the individuals from the original snap. Then Conti looked at his watch.

'We should go. We have one stop to make on our way.'

Jellicoe looked and asked 'Where?'

'Come with me.'

'Do you think this is one of the sicari that killed Meazza?'

Conti was too old a hand to answer conclusively. Instead he said, 'Your friend is in great danger. We must find him.'

'Then bring me to Cinecittà.'

'We will, but first I want you to meet someone; it's on our way,' said Conti handing over the photographs to Jellicoe that he and Panetta had extracted from the piles they had examined. Panetta, meanwhile, was once more rendering Rome traffic null and void with his distaste for driving sensibly. Jellicoe tried not to think about the near misses they were experiencing, focusing his attention on the pictures instead. This wasn't easy as the car was cornering as if it were on the raised banks of the Monza racetrack sending the two men in the back flying around the back seats. Perhaps there should be seat belts in the back, thought Jellicoe.

Photograph after photograph showed Sylvia smiling in the company of the Mateo de Luca. The extent of her betrayal revealed in some pictures that showed her dancing closely with the gang leader's son. Conti saw the pictures too but looked away, sensing the pain that Jellicoe would be feeling.

In this he was wrong. Much to his surprise he felt nothing, not even anger. It was if she was someone he had barely known, and this was probably true. If there was any pain it was the thought that he would like to have known the person in the photographs. She was beautiful, vivacious. He remembered someone like that, but it seemed like a long time ago.

Then he saw a man in the background of one of the photographs. Someone he knew. He felt the ghost of a chill. He was not with either Lentini or De Luca and yet he seemed as if he was part of the group. There was a connection there, Jellicoe felt sure of it.

'What is it?' asked Conti. Jellicoe pointed to the man. Conti frowned. "Are you sure?'

Jellicoe was silent for a moment while he tried to order his thoughts. It made no sense and yet it made complete sense. He was about to explain his thinking when he realised that the car had come to a stop and not as a consequence of piling into a lamp post.

The three men exited the car and climbed the steps into the building that housed the police. Jellicoe explained why he thought the man in the photograph should be brought in for questioning. Conti nodded and despatched Panetta to have men sent to pick him up.

Meanwhile, Jellicoe and Conti went downstairs into a basement floor where there were holding cells for people who were to be interviewed. The corridor had no natural light and felt claustrophobic to Jellicoe. Conti indicated the cell at the end of the corridor. A policeman jumped to his feet and stood to attention at the end of the corridor when he saw the commisario. Jellicoe tried to imagine Clarkey doing this with Burnett. It made him smile but only for a moment.

Conti arrived at the last door. He turned to Jellicoe and said, 'Look inside.'

Jellicoe slid back the shutter and gazed through the metal lattice bars. A man lay curled up on a bed. He could not see the face. Jellicoe glanced towards Conti and shrugged and took a look himself before instructing the policeman to open the cell door.

The door opened allowing the three policemen to enter the cell. Only then did the man stir from his position on the bed. He sat up and rubbed his eyes. Despite the messiness of his hair and the three days of growth of beard, Jellicoe recognised him immediately.

It was the other man in the photograph.

'Mr Jellicoe meet the man you have been looking for. His name is Tommaso Lupone. Or, perhaps, to give him his full title, Captain Tommaso Lupone, formerly ship's captain of the Silk Road. He's helping us with our questions.'

This comment was met with a scowl and a suggestion from Lupone that was explicit and anatomically impossible. Conti chuckled at the comment. He could afford to be magnanimous. After all, he would be leaving the cell while Lupone was facing a long time in just this sort of accommodation. Conti highlighted this to him as led Jellicoe out of the cell.

'Did you show the photograph I gave you.'

'I did but he's refusing to talk. For the moment, I should add. I must say Mr Jellicoe, your photograph is proving to be quite useful to us. It connects two men that we are interested in to a man that was clearly involved in transporting drugs around Europe. We have checked the ship's manifest, and it seems the Silk Road travels between France, Italy, Greece, and Britain.'

'You'll need more than this to convict Lentini or De Luca,' observed Jellicoe.

'True but if we can get Lupone to talk then, at least, we can begin to lay siege to their operation: names, dates, places and all the rest. Even if we can't reach the summit, we can scale a lot of the mountain and create the basis for conquest.'

'Are you a mountaineer by any chance?' asked Jellicoe, with a smile as they walked back down the corridor.

'I am merely an enthusiastic amateur. Now, I think we should go to Cinecittà and intercept your commanding officer before he gets into too much trouble.'

They left the cell to find Panetta waiting. Jellicoe groaned inwardly. He was holding car keys.

22

One hour earlier:

The taxi driver turned to greet his new passenger. The taxi driver was called Enrico and had been named after Enrico Ottavo, or as he is better known in England, Henry VIII. His father was an Anglophile and taught history at school. Young Enrico proved a disappointment academically but had a very strong sense of direction. That sense of direction took him out of the school gates and into a taxi. He'd been a driver for twenty years and enjoyed his work immensely. He loved meeting new customers, many had become regular, some had become friends and on a few very serendipitous occasions even lovers. The stories he could tell and if the journey were long enough, he would.

'Dov'e?' asked Enrico with a broad and welcoming smile. His new customer was foreign, that much was clear and surprisingly well-dressed.

Burnett's mind was racing after having seen Jellicoe arrested. What on earth had happened? It was one thing to be poking their noses into matters that were most certainly outside their jurisdiction but to be arrested for it? That Jellicoe had been arrested was not even a question in Burnett's mind. He thought quickly. He needed to find someone who spoke

English. The face that floated into his mind was that of Culver Wendell. What was the name of Culver's newspaper. He took a stab at it.

'Courier,' said Burnett hopefully. This was met with a blank look by the Enrico, the taxi driver. Burnett turned around. Three policemen were sprinting towards the taxi. Burnett made an opening and closing gesture with his hands. 'Courier,' he said frantically.

For some reason this did seem to land with the taxi driver. Moments later they sped off just as the three policemen were upon them. For a few moments, Burnett was feeling a little bit more chipper about having communicated in Italian, the driver said, 'Dov'e?'

Burnett looked into the eyes of the taxi driver in his rear-view mirror.

'Polizia e andata.'

Burnett did not need to speak Italian to work out that the taxi driver had helped him escape. He had, however, learned at least one word in Italian.

'Grazie,' said Burnett. They drove along Via Veneto then turned off in case the police were following them. At one point Burnett had the driver stop. He leapt out and bought a copy of the Corriere d'Informazione. He showed it to the taxi driver and pointed to the title.

'Offices,' said Burnett hoping that it sounded a little like the Italian version of the word.

'Ahh, ufficio, si,' said the taxi driver.

At this point Burnett was thrown back into his seat as Enrico put his foot to the floor.

'Bloody hell,' said Burnett or something approximating this. They arrived at the Rome offices of the newspaper in a matter of minutes.

'Grazie,' said a relieved Burnett, handing over some money to Enrico. He wondered if he should ask the driver to stay but then thought better of it. Life was too short, at least it would be if he risked another journey like the one he'd just had.

He walked through the doors conscious that everyone's eyes were on him. This was not unusual given his profession, but it was the first time he'd received such attention for the way he was dressed. He strode over to the reception and asked for Culver Wendell. The man on reception looked at him coolly and then consulted a list in front of him. Then he picked up a phone and rang a number.

'Ciao. C'e un uomo to vuole; si chiama Burnett.' The receptionist had to repeat the name a couple of times before it was understood. It was for strange for Burnett to hear his name so badly mangled. He wondered how badly English people distorted foreign words when they attempted to communicate in the local language. The receptionist handed the phone to Burnett.

'Hello Culver, it's Nick Jellicoe's friend, Reg Burnett.'

'Hiya Reg, what's cookin'?' said the American.

'Nick might be. He was arrested earlier by Commisario Conti. Look, I may need your help.'

'Are you down in reception?'

'Yes.'

'On my way. I'll see you outside.'

This struck Burnett as odd, but he was in no position to argue the point with the American. He handed the phone back to the receptionist and headed back outside of the building.

After the cool of the reception area, the heat outside hit him like a blast furnace. He went in search of some shade.

Culver appeared a few minutes later. He did a double take when he saw what Burnett was wearing.

'That must have been some night out you had,' said Culver with a smile but he was evidently worried too. 'What happened?'

Culver led Burnett towards a bar that would allow then to sit down in the shade. They ordered two espressos and then Burnett updated Culver on what they had done that day leading up to what he'd seen at the hotel.

'You're sure he was being arrested Reg?'

'Trust me son, I've arrested enough people to know what it looks like. I have no idea why.'

'Look, you stay here and let me make some phone calls. I'll try and find out what's going on.'

'There's one more thing Culver. Nick was meant to meet this chap Carlo Meazza at Cinecittà today. I've no idea if he speaks English. Do you still have the photo Nick gave you of his wife with those Mafia boys?'

'It's at my desk. I'll bring it down. Give me ten or fifteen minutes and I'll find out what's up.'

'Thanks,' replied Burnett. He watched the American rise from his seat and stride purposefully back towards the offices of the newspaper. Fifteen minutes turned into half an hour and three more espressos for Burnett. This had the exactly the impact that four espressos in the space of forty minutes would have on anyone not of an Italian disposition. Burnett's eyes were wide, and his mind was spinning with possibilities that might have led to Jellicoe's arrest. He had arrived at seven different scenarios and counting when the American arrived back accompanied by Marilyn the bulldog. None were correct.

'You said you were going to meet Carlo Meazza?'

'Yes,' answered Burnett. 'You're not saying he's the killer. That can't be right. He's just a snapper. Maybe he...'

Culver held up his hand to stop Burnett's train of thought heading off the rails and onto the platform. He noted the three empty cups which suggested that the Englishman was jacked up to his eyeballs on caffeine.

'There's been a murder, but my contact doesn't know who. Who have you seen today?'

'We saw Geno Muro, the photographer,' answered Burnett.

'Maybe he's the one that was killed,' suggested Culver.

'That can't be right Culver,' said Burnett and even he was conscious of how quickly he was talking. 'When we left him he seemed alive to me, Culver.'

'Well the poor guy's dead now, by the sound of it. Paolo Nesta is on his way down here he wants to chat to you.'

'Sure Culver. Shall we get another espresso while we're waiting?'

Culver's short reply suggested that Burnett should not consider another one for twelve hours at least. Thankfully, Nesta arrived before Burnett, true to character, went into full rebellion mode.

Nesta joined them at the table and was on the point of ordering a coffee when he saw Culver shake his head slowly and indicate the three empty cups by Burnett. A smile crossed his face but faded quickly. He updated the two men on his latest call.

'I spoke with my contact at the police. Someone was shot today and at the moment the police have Nick, and they are looking everywhere for you.'

'That's not good,' said Burnett, his eyes darting left and right in case any policeman should be in the vicinity.

'I did hear something else, too. Was there a drugs raid last night in Ostia?'

'They did it. That's great, Paolo. I'm happy for Conti. He seems like a good man. Have you known him long?'

Nesta held up his hand to stop Burnett's train of thought which was going faster than a Ferrari and certainly more rapidly than the Italian could keep up with notwithstanding his excellent English.

'Slow down, Chief Inspector. Can you tell me what you know about the drugs raid.'

'It was Nick.'

The two journalists turned to each other and then back to Burnett.

'Go on.'

'Yes, it was Nick. He tipped them off.'

'How?' asked Nesta.

'He received a telegram. He thinks it was from his mother-in-law. It said there was a boat called the Silk Road leaving Ostia bound for England loaded with drugs. Did they catch them? That's great. It really is,' rambled Burnett. He picked up one of the espresso cups to drain anything that was left in the bottom. 'Are you sure you don't want a coffee?'

'No,' chorused the two journalists before Culver added, 'Tell us what happened earlier.'

Thanks to precise questioning from Nesta, the fired-up Burnett was kept under a firm leash and the story was related.

All the time, Nesta recorded everything in his notebook. This was going to be quite a scoop for him. It had been a while since he'd had one of those. Of late his energy had not been what it was or perhaps it was a lurking fear of offending someone he should not, on either side of the law. Around three, Burnett's eyes widened, and he grabbed Culver's arm.

'Do you have the photo, Culver? I need to get to Cinecittà.'

Despite being oddly impressed by the pronunciation in which Burnett had correctly turned the second 'c' into a 'ch', Nesta was curious about why he needed to be there.

'I have to meet Carlo Meazza,' said Burnett. He's expecting Nick and me at four. That guy Silvio organised it for us. He wants the story. You and Silvio will have to arm wrestle over that one Paolo, old son,' cackled Burnett.

'Arm wrestle?' said Nesta, a little confused.

'Never mind,' replied Culver. 'Let's take your car, Paolo.'

A few minutes later they were standing by Nesta's car. Burnett looked distinctly unimpressed with the mode of transport.

'Call that a car?'

The beige-coloured Fiat 500 looked as if it could barely cope with one full-grown man never mind three. Burnett, Culver and Nesta were on the large side of large while Marilyn the bulldog had long since given up looking after her figure. Nesta waved him off with a laugh and said something very like nonsense with his hand.

The three men squeezed into the tiny Fiat without having, as Burnett suggested, to stick limbs out of the window. Soon they were zipping along Via Tuscolana towards the enormous film studio. Marilyn was on the backseat with the Englishman. Burnett and Marilyn spent the entire journey eyeing one another suspiciously. At one point Culver spotted this and said laughingly, 'Were you two separated at birth, chief?'

This was met by a growl from both the policeman and Marilyn which suggested some truth in the original proposition.

The benefit of the Fiat 500 became apparent even to the espresso-frazzled mind of Burnett when they arrived at the film studio. Nesta parked in a space so tiny that a mouse would have complained of claustrophobia. As they exited the car, Burnett walked to the front and the back of the car to observe that the bumpers of the Fiat were touching the cars either side of them. He shook his head and followed the two journalists to the entrance of Cinecittà.

Cinecittà was built by Mussolini's Fascists in the decade before the war. The fascist style of architecture took design cues from Ancient Rome; they were very large, symmetrical with sharp non-rounded edges. The buildings were designed to convey a sense of awe and intimidation through their size and were made of limestone and other durable stones in order to last the entirety of the fascist era and create impressive ruins. Cinecittà combined a little of this with the prevailing art deco aesthetic that was popular in the period.

At the door of the film studio was Fabrizio Bellini, a man for whom Italy's golden age was slowly being frittered away by a new generation of sodomists and pederasts. Quite why he had chosen a career that gave him daily exposure to both was beyond the comprehension of the many writers, artists and technicians whose misfortune it was to pass his sour face day after day. In Bellini's view Italy's golden age did not include either the Roman empire or even the Renaissance. No, Bellini was a Fascist to his fingertips and cried the day Mussolini met his end hanging upside down in the small village of Giulino di Mezzegra in northern Italy.

'He was a hero,' he would say to anyone that was listening and by now, nobody was. Bellini would long ago have been handed his cards were it not for a fact that he was a member of a union of the sort that he purported to despise because they undermined the vigour of the nation by protecting sub-standard workers. The irony was of course lost on man whose belief system was devoid of such nuance.

Bellini stepped out of his gatehouse and stood in front of the entrance like a warrior on the bridge at Thermopylae. He stared at the new arrivals with barely disguised contempt. He didn't like foreigners and had already perceived that two of the men and the ridiculous canine were not pure-blooded Italians. Nesta, a communist, which is to say he was mildly left of centre, could spot a Fascist at a thousand paces. Something in the pencil moustache, the slicked back hair, the sharpness of the crease in his trousers and the unconcealed expression of hatred towards his fellow man marked this middle-aged individual standing in front of the entrance out as a former, current and future follower of Mussolini and his like. Nesta knew how to deal with men like this.

'Have you your police identification?' whispered Nesta to Burnett from the side of his mouth as they were still around twenty metres from the gate.

As it happened, Burnett did although, strictly speaking he should not have brought it over to Italy. A nod to Nesta then the journalist moved ahead of Burnett and received identification like a relay runner receiving a baton. He flashed it before the suspicious eyes of Bellini.

'Police, we've come to interview Carlo Meazza,' said Nesta.

Meazza, in Bellini's eyes, symbolised everything that was turning his country into a sewer. Him and his friends were not only undermining the morals of what used to be a Catholic country through their licentious behaviour, but he also suspected them of being drug users of the very worst kind. The policeman before him seemed to have the seriousness and the gravitas to understand the peril Italy was facing since they'd lost Il Duce. It was only by a whisker, as he let them through, that he restrained himself from offering a supportive straight-armed salute so beloved of Fascist the world over.

'These men are from Interpol,' said Nesta as he marched through the gate, eyes straight ahead.

Interpol thought Bellini. I knew it. Drugs. He wanted to share his suspicions on the subject to this impressive mam, but he was already on his way ahead marching with purpose towards the reception building. Perhaps later, he thought.

Around fifteen minutes later, Bellini was once more called into action as a group of men approached. This time there was no question who they were. The police car was something of a giveaway. As he saw them, it occurred to Bellini in a moment of unusual and not-to-be-repeated insight that the other policemen had been driving a Fiat 500. This was somewhat unusual leading Bellini to surmise they were running an undercover operation.

The man leading the group gave Bellini a momentary thrill of pride. This was a leader. A man not just among men but a lion among sheep. The firm line of the jaw, the glint of stone in his eye. Yes, this was a leader. Bellini stepped back and could not stop himself saluting this man in the only way he knew how.

189

Conti saw Bellini offer the Fascist salute and was unsure if this was an attempt at mockery. Panetta was in no doubt and was about to launch into a firm denunciation of everything despotic when he saw Conti hold his hand up. Like Nesta he'd sized up Bellini in a moment.

'Where can I find Carlo Meazza?'

'The other men have gone to arrest him already.'

Conti blanched at this. Men? Arrest? He turned to Jellicoe in the hope that he might provide an explanation to the growing insanity he was having to deal with. Jellicoe smiled and offered a shrug. He'd understood the same as Conti. Men? Arrest? It occurred to him at that moment that perhaps Burnett, rather intelligently, had called upon the help of Culver Wendell.

'Let's go,' said Conti, not waiting any longer.

Bellini smiled at the policemen as they entered but stopped when he saw Jellicoe. The face was familiar. Wasn't he an English actor? Was he under arrest too? The whole gang of pederasts and drug takers was being rounded up. His heart began to swell with pride. Perhaps, just perhaps his country was going to be rescued from the cesspit into which it was sinking.

And he, Fabrizio Bellini would not stand idly by and let these brave policemen tackle this virus on their own. He returned to the gatehouse. Inside the top drawer he kept a souvenir from the days when he was doing his bit to make Italy great again. The revolver was antique, but he kept it in excellent working order. Taking it out from the drawer he gazed at it appreciatively. Then, with determination raging like a fire in his eyes, he abandoned his post and made his way towards the studio.

In doing so, he missed the seeing another man walking in the direction of the entrance to the film studio. Inside his pocket was a police identification. It was fake. He stopped and stared in disbelief at the security man leaving his post with what looked like a gun in his hand. Deciding it had to be an unrelated matter he started moving again towards the unguarded entrance. Not for him the need to go to reception. He knew the film studio very well. He knew where Carlo Meazza was meant to be. The arrival of the policemen was a complication, of course, but this manageable.

Hadn't it always been so?

23

Music was playing from somewhere. While Burnett was no fan of rock n' roll he wasn't entirely unaware of its existence of its leading exponents. The Everly Brothers were being played in one of the large studio lots surrounding the reception building. If he could hear it from outside he could only begin to imagine how loud it must be inside.

They walked into the reception of Cinecittà. Paolo Nesta still had Burnett's police identification as back up in case they met with any interference from power-crazy receptionists.

The young woman on reception, unlike Bellini was a model of cooperation as well as, in Burnett's view, a model in real life. As they walked out of the reception in the direction the young woman had suggested, Burnett posed the question that he had first considered when he'd been on Via Veneto for the first time.

'Do you Italians know how lucky you are?'

Nesta laughed but then considered the question at face value.

'It's true we have great weather, the best food in the world, Roma is the most beautiful city in the world, we have the best art, we invented opera. Was there anything else you had in mind?' asked the journalist with a wicked grin.

'No,' said Burnett glumly which made Nesta's grin stretch even wider. They were heading towards the lot where the music was playing. 'Sounds like the party is in full swing.'

It transpired that Meazza was probably attending a party taking place in one of the lots to celebrate the end of shooting. Burnett had no clue as to what Nesta and the young woman had been talking about other than that she had pointed vaguely in the direction of some building or another. He followed along with nest and Culver who was unusually quiet. Marilyn was beginning to breathe heavily. She was not designed for walking long distances. Or short distances either, for that matter.

'It's a big place,' observed Burnett wiping the perspiration from his forehead.

Music continued to echo from one of the big lots. It took five minutes to walk from the reception, but they finally made it to the large, enclosed building where the music was playing. Burnett recognised the song although this was an Italian version of one of his favourite Dean Martin tracks, 'Mambo Italian (Nel blu dipinto di blu)'. The lot had large sliding doors at the gable end. They entered through those.

The music was louder now but Burnett could also hear lots of voices. There was laugher and chatter. All of this was taking place on the other side of large wooden structures with timber supports. Men and women milling around these clutching glasses of champagne. It was not yet four in the afternoon. Burnett admired their style.

When they rounded the corner of the structure, Burnet's mouth fell open. There in front of him was Via Veneto, recreated inside the enormous lot. He saw the bars that he and Jellicoe had visited recreated with astonishing exactitude. There were no cars on this street just dozens of men and women either sitting chatting or dancing; others were smoking and drinking. A plume of smoke was floating over the scene partially obscuring the studio lights that illuminated the street.

'Pretty impressive,' said Culver with a grin. Marilyn was attracting the attention of some young women who strolled over to greet the bulldog.

'Pretty impressive all right,' agreed Burnett only he wasn't talking about the set.

Nesta was the least enthralled by what he saw. He was casting his eyes around looking for the man they come to see. He turned to see that Culver was now chatting with two young women while Burnett was in the process of taking a drink from a tray offered by a young man in a waiter's costume.

'I will look for Meazza,' shouted Nesta over the din of the music.

Burnett gave him the thumbs up. Culver, too, was holding a drink and seemed to have lost all interest in the purpose of their visit. As Nesta wandered off, Burnett decided to explore a little of the film set. Now that he was in the middle of it all he could see that the full street had not been recreated, just one section. It was a bar with tables and chairs outside rather like the ones he'd sat on over the previous two nights.

He walked along set in the manner of a tourist, spinning every so often in an effort to take everything in. He'd never been to a film set before and it was a fascinating sight. On one side was the large structure recreating the bars and the other was the lights, the cameras and other equipment. It was a monumental undertaking from what he could see. He'd never be able to look at a film again at the cinema without having a greater appreciation of what it required.

Burnett was nimble as galleon at the best of times, on his bumbling around the set, he brushed rather heavily past a petite young woman with honey-coloured hair. She turned sharply to him. Dark brown eyes scalded Burnett. He smiled an apology and continued walking. It was only a few paces later he realised that the woman he'd bumped into had been staring down at him from billboards and magazine covers. What was her name? Burnett couldn't recall. He moved on until he reached the end of the street

There were a number of smaller interior sets. They were lit up and crowded with people who looked as if they were at a dinner party. Just how many people did it take to make a film? Burnett stopped and set his drink down on the tray of a passing waiter. He helped himself to another glass of champagne.

The combination of the champagne bubbles and the numerous espressos he'd had earlier were beginning to tell even on a constitution as robust as Burnett's. his head was spinning a little and when he started walking again, his gait was a little less steady that normal.

He headed towards a set made to look like a living room. It was like no living room he'd ever been in before. How the other half lived he thought. Everyone appeared to be having a good time. A couple of men were sitting on a sofa in a manner that might have raised an eyebrow or seven at The Hen and Chicken. On another seat a man sat alone contentedly smoking what was certainly not a cigarette or a cigar. At his feet was another man, unconscious but still clutching onto his glass of champagne as though his life depended on it.

He entered a highly realistic kitchen, so realistic in fact that he tried one of the taps. It didn't work. The sink was doubling up as a dumping ground for some bottles and cigarette butts.

All around were empty glasses, smashed glasses and God is good, a full glass because he'd just drained his. He looked around and established that it had no owner. He walked away with it and began to head back in the direction that he'd come from.

When he arrived back he realised that there was no sign of either Paolo Nesta or Culver. He stood for a while unsure of what to do then an idea struck him. Perhaps if he could find the girl he'd bumped into earlier then she would be with the man who had made her a star, Carlo Meazza.

He moved forward through a thicket of people that were moving their bodies in a manner that suggested they were dancing or experiencing a fit, Burnett could not make up his mind. He stumbled past them and spotted the young woman again. She was with two men that even to Burnett's ingenuous eyes were unlikely to have much interest in her.

As he approached it occurred to him that she might not speak English. The young woman stared at the approaching Burnett with something approaching revulsion. To her he was yet another lecherous old man bolstered by booze making his attack.

Burnett had no idea what she was thinking beyond the sinking realisation that his approach was unwelcome. He tried smiling but even he accepted that his days of charming young women with a cheeky grin dated back to before the war.

'Carlo Meazza?' said Burnett. The alcohol had helped his accent no end and he could see that the young woman had understood him. She shrugged, turned and pointed to an older man standing beside yet another stunning young woman. He'd missed his calling, decided Burnett. In the next life he would work in films.

196

'Carlo Meazza?' repeated Burnett to the man who had turned around.

The man's brow furrowed a little. He looked away from Burnett and scanned the throng of people on the studio lot. His head began to shake a little.

'American?'

'English,' said Burnett who unaccountably stood a little bit more erect when he said this as if his previously slouched posture was somehow letting the side down.

'I have not seen Carlo. He should be here today.'

Thankful to meet someone who spoke English, Burnett gestured in the general direction of the partygoers.

'What's going on?'

'You don't know?' asked the man with a smile. It occurred to Burnett that the man was a little bit tipsy. Not unlike himself, he realised. 'It is a 'wrap' party I think you say. Federico has finally finished the film.'

The man pointed to a small clapper board, like a child's version of the real thing. It read: F. Fellini. La Dolce Vita. Prod. Riama Film. Burnett picked it up.

'Take it,' said the man. 'Sorry I cannot help you.'

Burnett nodded to him and put the souvenir in his inside breast pocket and continued on his way. He needed to find Nesta and Culver but there was no sign of them. He walked away from the throng back towards one of the other smaller interior sets.

The combination of the espressos earlier, the champagne, the strange smell from the smoke and the loud music was beginning to tell on him. His head was spinning he was not used to even after a particularly convivial evening spent with

Clarkey and Crumbs. He needed to sit down and take stock of the situation.

He swayed a little as he walked towards an empty sofa. His throat felt drier than a temperance hall. He looked around for some water. Aside from a vase with some flowers in it, there wasn't much on offer. Then from behind him he heard a voice call his name.

'Reg, is that you?' Burnett turned around and saw the American friend of Culver. He stood up, somewhat unsteadily, and shook the American's hand.

'Hello there, Dino, what are you doing here?'

'I got a call from my boss, you met him, Mr Di Nozzi. He asked me to help out here today at the party. He's hoping a few of them will come over later to Harry's Bar and spend some money. I said sure thing so here I am.'

'I'm with Culver, he's here somewhere,' explained Burnett.

Dino was surprised by this. He said, 'Really? He didn't say nothing to me.'

'Long story. It was last minute. Have you seen this photographer we're after, Carlo Meazza.'

'I've no idea what he looks like, Reg. Hey are you ok. You look a little...'

'Sozzled?' laughed Burnett. 'I think I went a bit heavy on the champagne here.'

'Let me get you some water. In fact, Reg, why don't you come with me. I'll find you some water and we'll see if we can find Culver anywhere.'

'Good idea,' agreed Burnett. 'Lead on Macduff.'

24

If the receptionist was surprised to see yet another group of policemen who were interested in the policemen who had come asking for Carlo Meazza then she certainly showed it. Alarm spread across her face like a wildfire in a forest. Who had she let in in?

'But they showed me identification,' she said alarmed that she would be in trouble.

Conti held his hand up to stop the veritable torrent of self-justification from the young woman.

'Yes, I'm sure they had identification. Where did they go?'

The young woman was about to continue her non-apologetic apology when she suddenly sensed the urgency in Conti's eyes. She pointed in the direction of a large studio lot.

'Go to where the music is coming from. They are having a 'wrap' party.'

The three policemen immediately left the reception area. They heard the sounds of music blaring from one of the large buildings. No one spoke. They walked quickly towards the building. Around fifty yards behind them, unseen, was Fabrizio Bellini half running, half walking in order to keep up. One hand was free, the other was in his pocket, caressing the antique revolver.

It took a couple of minutes, but they arrived at the same spot that Burnett and the others had arrived at ten minutes earlier in front of the large lot. Jellicoe looked at his watch. It was just after five to four.

Screams and laughter intermingled with the music. It sounded as if there were a lot of people inside the lot. Jellicoe turned to Conti and said, 'Should we split up?'

Conti thought for a few moments then said, 'No. we'll see what it's like inside first then we can decide.'

They moved the large side entrance and walked towards the large wooden construction. Once past it they took in a section of Via Veneto that had been built for the film. Jellicoe was impressed by what he saw. It seemed more real than the street itself. There were dozens of people in front of them and it was virtually impossible to make anyone out that they might recognise.

'Yes we separate,' agreed Conti. 'If we find the chief inspector then we should meet back at this point.'

'Perhaps we should come back in here in fifteen minutes anyway,' said Jellicoe, scanning the lot.

'Agreed,' said Conti. 'And if you see...'

'Don't worry,' said Jellicoe, 'I have no intention of being stabbed.'

They moved forward together towards the street then at a certain point Jellicoe moved along the left-hand side where the bars and the outdoor tables where located while Conti walked along the reconstructed street itself. Panetta took the right where the cameras and the equipment would have been placed for shooting the street scenes.

Jellicoe's mind was racing in tandem with his heart. The folly of what he had done was becoming all too clear. He had put not just himself at risk but also a man he liked and respected. Why had he put them all in such danger? Redemption barely seemed credible. Sylvia had not deserved her fate but nor was the memory of their time together sufficient to justify the extraordinary peril he had placed Burnett in by this foolish adventure. Did he really think he could take on organised crime in Italy; single-handedly?

Then there was Claudia. She had used him. Of this there was no question. He had been a pawn in a larger game she was playing. First, by getting him to put the crime bosses on alert that they were being investigated and then by using him as a glorified messenger boy for her casual dismantling of the drug smuggling operation that had almost certainly killed her daughter and husband. She was after revenge, and she'd had it. Or had she? Was there still another move left in this game?

He moved forward slowly between the bar fronts and the outdoor tables. Glancing over to his right he saw Conti and further up, Panetta, moving in parallel, like three gunslingers walking up main street.

As he walked, he became aware of a group sitting at the table who went silent as he neared them. Out of his peripheral vision he had the uncomfortable feeling they were all looking at him. Jellicoe glanced down and his eyes were immediately, and inevitably, drawn to a beautiful blonde woman who was staring at him with a look of amazement on her face. He recognised her but could not quite put a name to her face. The man beside her he did recognise. It was Federico Fellini. There was no question they were talking about him. The expression on the face of the Italian director was somewhere between surprise and amusement. By the time Jellicoe remembered the name of the actress and why she seemed so taken aback he was already past them.

The table all at once broke into excited chat. What was it Oscar Wilde said about the one thing in life worse than being talked about, and that is not being talked about. Jellicoe was convinced he would be the subject of their conversation for at least the next few seconds. Fame at last.

There was no sign of Burnett, though. He glanced over towards the other two policemen. They were looking in his direction too. Conti shrugged. They had reached the end of the street. He indicated with his hand that he would retrace his footsteps but suggested that Panetta and Jellicoe pushed forwards and examine the smaller interiors further up.

Where was Burnett?

*

Burnett was now at the far end of the lot, just past the last interior set. It was much darker here, but the cacophony echoed all the way around them. It was giving him a headache. He really needed that water. His mood rather matched his feelings about the investigation. Things were going downhill fast. He returned to thinking about what he had witnessed earlier at the hotel. Could he have misunderstood what had happened? It made no sense that Jellicoe, and by extension him, were suspects.

'Sit here, Reg,' said Dino. 'I'll go find you some water.'

Something had clearly happened that had made Conti act in the way he had. Burnett considered things from a different angle. Rather than arresting Jellicoe, had Conti been, in fact, acting to remove him forcibly from the investigation? There had to be a reason for this that went beyond what they had done so far. It could be he was acting on instructions coming from on high, either in Italy or even from home. Or had something else happened of which they were not aware. Had the drugs raid been a success? Or a bust? If it were the latter then Burnett could see that he and Jellicoe would be on a very sticky wicket.

He glanced at his watch. It was almost four and he was parched. Where was Dino? A part of him wanted to get up and recommence his search for Meazza but his legs just weren't up to it. He was exhausted, drained of all feeling, the enthusiasm for the chase had slowly been sapped. The last few days were catching up on him. In truth, he wanted to return home now, an empty home but home all the same. He closed his eyes for a moment. Just to rest them, he thought. Why did people keep disappearing on him?

He opened them a moment later as he sensed someone approach. He turned around and tried clear the muzziness away. The light was too dim to make out who it was. The man was silhouetted against the studio lights further down the lot.

Then he saw the unmistakeable glint of steel: a knife. A rather large one too. The man moved noiselessly, swiftly like a blur towards him. Burnett lowered his head and tried to fling himself at the attacker, catch him by surprise, but it felt as if were moving through treacle. The stabbing pain when it came was unbearable. It was in the side of his chest. He fell to the ground and heard a grunt but wasn't sure if it was him or the phantom. It felt as if every last article of air had escaped his body and in its place was a burning agony. Fighting for breath, Burnett tried to rise to his feet but collapsed on his face.

Then everything went dark.

25

It was Conti who ran into Paolo Nesta first. Literally. Neither were looking where they were going and bumped together. Just as they were apologising they recognised one another. The apology died on their lips to be followed by a fleeting, crinkling smile on both men. Nesta had always quite liked Conti. There was an authority about him, integrity, too. Conti was a dying species; a bit like him. Both wanted so much to see their country escape the stigma of the last war and take their place at the forefront of a united and peaceful Europe. Instead, they were being held back by a toxic legacy that dated back to long before the war: organised crime and corruption.

'Have you seen the Englishman?' asked Conti urgently.

'Burnett?' asked Nesta

'Yes,' responded Conti sharply.

'I've lost him. I told him to wait at the top of the street while I looked for Meazza.'

'Meazza's dead,' shouted Conti as the music seemed to become, if anything, louder. They were standing in the middle of the recreated Via Veneto and were being jostled by people who were dancing wildly to Elvis Presley.

By mutual consent they moved off the street allowing Conti to update the journalist on what had happened. Nesta leaned in to hear Conti better.

'Do you think the killer might be here?'

Conti shrugged and replied, 'He might be if he thinks that the two Englishmen are a threat. All I want to do is find them and put them on a plane. They've been useful but enough is enough. I want them to go.'

The two men walked along the other side of the street that Panetta had recently been on. They returned to the spot that Nesta had originally parted company from Culver and Burnett.

'I left them here.'

'Them?'

'Culver Wendell, he's an American journalist who lives here. Do you know him?'

The expression on Conti's face confirmed he had no idea who he was. Conti was unsure of what to do now. The studio lot was very crowded and seeing anyone amongst the throng of faces was proving very difficult. It all felt like a waste of time when he had the murder of Meazza and the capture of the men from the Silk Road to be dealing with. There was no question now. He needed to be rid of the two men from England.

*

Jellicoe was becoming increasingly alarmed by the absence of Burnett. His mood was not helped by the fact that there were so many people around him who appeared to have neither a capacity for alcohol nor any spatial awareness if the number of people bashing into him was any guide. Quite a few people were comatose now, but this may not have been solely the fault of the alcohol. It seemed to Jellicoe that quite a few of the partygoers were smoking marijuana. Certainly, the smell in some areas was quite overpowering.

He was now past Via Veneto and searching through some of the interior sets. There was still no sign of Burnett. Jellicoe felt a pain in the palm of his hand. He realised that the fist he was making meant he was digging his nails into his hand. He blamed himself for the mess they were in.

Pushing forward he moved his head from left to right like a clock's pendulum. Up ahead he saw that it was much darker, so he decided to ignore the interiors and see what was at the far end of the lot where there were no lights or sets.

There was no escape from the music still. It carried and pinballed off the walls as if were trying to escape. He passed a couple that were probably seconds away from committing an act that was entirely legal in a house but probably an offence in public. In fact, there were more than one couple in advanced stages of shedding clothes, inhibitions and any sense of propriety. He might have felt envious were it not for the fact that fear was gripping him now. Not for himself but for Burnett. The sense of guilt deepened with every step along with an impending sense that he was too late.

*

Fabrizio Bellini was appalled by what he saw taking place inside the lot. His conviction that his country was descending into a cesspit of sex and degradation was increasing with every step that he took along the recreated Via Veneto. This conviction was matched on in intensity by his anger. He gripped the gun which he no longer sought to hide more tightly. A few people saw him, looked down at the gun and laughed manically. Drunk, he thought. Would any jury convict him if he leased off a few rounds into this Gomorrah? At least it might put an end to the cacophony coming from the speakers.

His eyes alighted on Jellicoe. The man was alone. He had escaped the police officer. This was his chance to his duty for his country. He would apprehend the foreigner. He marched forward, his eyes fixed on Jellicoe.

A few people now, less drunk, saw what Bellini was carrying and ducked out of his way. It was like a Red Sea parting for him. Jellicoe was in his sights, and he would not escape. A flinty smile crossed his lips. He felt like a cacciatore, a hunter.

*

Something was wrong. Every fibre of Jellicoe was telling him that he should have encountered Burnett by now or one of the men he was with. More and more he was encountering men and women lying on the ground either taking an opportunity to sleep off the effects of what they had been consuming or taking advantage of the same with a like-minded partner.

He damned himself for his careless disregard for his and Burnett's safety. A man bumped into him, and Jellicoe shoved him forcefully out of the way. This was greeted with an angry shout. Just as Jellicoe turned to respond, he saw out of the corner of his eye a man crouching over a body. He was twenty yards away and it was difficult to make out who the two were but there was no mistaking the sight of the blood on the white shirt.

Then he saw who was kneeling. It was Dino, the American they had met the previous night. Dino stood up and looked around him wildly. There was blood on his hands. Jellicoe glanced down at the man lying on the ground. Nausea rose within him as he realised it was Burnett.

Just as he was about to rush towards Burnett he felt something a jab of steel in his side. It propelled him forward slightly. Jellicoe spun around to find himself staring down the muzzle of a pistol. The man holding the pistol was looking slightly deranged. It took a moment to place him before Jellicoe realised he was looking at the doorman they had encountered when they arrived at the film studio.

Fabrizio Bellini was no one's fool. He'd watched enough John Wayne films to know that standing to close to a man when you have a gun is an open invitation to be disarmed. Having alerted his quarry to the fact that he was caught, he stepped back and kept his gun trained on Jellicoe's body.

'Hand's up,' said Bellini, indicating with his gun.

Jellicoe could not believe what was happening. What did this idiot think he was doing? Unless he was the sicaro. One look at Bellini's wild-eyed mania was enough to convince Jellicoe that he was not looking at cold-blooded hitman. This man was an idiot. A dangerous idiot.

Jellicoe pointed behind him.

'A man has been hurt. He needs a doctor,' said Jellicoe in Italian.

Bellini's eyes shifted towards the prone body of Burnett. There was large patch of blood on his white shirt. Even Bellini's rather limited intellect was capable of understanding that the man was seriously hurt, and that Jellicoe could not have been responsible. The man needed a doctor, and quickly. He lowered the gun just as he felt a sharp pain in the back of his head.

Jellicoe eyes followed the gun being lowered then, to his amazement, Bellini suddenly crumpled to the ground. A man that Jellicoe had neither seen nor heard bent down and picked up the gun. The man rose up with the gun in his hand. It was pointed, once more, at Jellicoe.

Now there could be no doubt. This was the man he was looking for. The sicaro known as Il Cacciatore. The man who had led him here and would now kill him. The man who had killed Burnett. The man who had killed Sylvia. The blood rushing around Jellicoe's head was a savage roar; the nausea rose like a tidal wave within him. He could almost taste the bitterness in his mouth. He would die ingloriously. He would die like his wife, at the hands of this man.

He would die.

Their eyes were fixed on one another. It was a gesture, nothing more, but at that moment it meant everything.

'Well, come on,' snarled Jellicoe. 'What are you waiting for?' He couldn't bring himself to say the man's name. The man he'd met only the previous day. The man he'd seen in the photograph of Carlo Meazza's. He hoped Conti would follow up on him after he was dead.

What was he waiting for? He would never have a better chance than now to do what he wanted to do. All of Jellicoe's senses were alive now. The smell of stale marijuana, the sound of the Italian singer, Mina playing on the speakers, the shouts, the laughter, the screams of the partygoers. He heard all of it with perfect clarity, and then he heard another type of shouting. It was different in tone and timber to the other noises. People were coming.

The man Jellicoe knew as Silvio raised the gun. He shrugged slightly. The music had stopped now which was clearly an inconvenience for the hitman. His eyes flicked in the direction of where they had been playing the music.

'I'm sorry,' said Silvio, 'You're getting too close to the truth. It's not personal.'

A thin smile crossed Jellicoe's face. He said, 'It certainly feels that way from here.'

'I would have left you alone. After the drugs raid they told me you had to be stopped. You shouldn't have done that.'

There was a moment of silence between them. Jellicoe could hear his heart beating. Each second was a countdown to when the music would begin and then he would join Burnett. He wondered idly what was holding up the music.

'I suppose you will write about this in your magazine,' said Jellicoe. 'Il Cacciatore strikes again. Who is this mysterious sicaro?'

Silvio's face was grave. This was a man who clearly did not enjoy his work. 'Of course,' replied the hitman, 'but you and Mr Burnett will be front cover. I won't mention the ridiculous name.'

Jellicoe looked unimpressed. He said, 'I'm honoured.' The music started up again. It was 'Nel blue, dipinto di blu' by Domenico Mondugno.

Jellicoe could sense the hitman or the journalist or whatever he was gently pulling the trigger. Then suddenly Silvio's head jerked to the right. Like Bellini moments before, he crumpled to the ground.

Dead.

26

Three weeks later

London: September 1959

'Joe, I have it,' Barry Cooper, arriving in the pub. As if to prove this he brandished a piece of paper and waved it from of the face of his friend Joe Sanders. handed his friend Joe Sanders a piece of paper. Sanders looked up from his pint of ale and grinned. He snatched the piece of paper from Cooper. The two men were in a pub in Walthamstow in London. It was early evening, yet the pub was mobbed with men. There were no women on this side of the bar.

'Let me see,' said Sanders leaning forward and nearly spilling his drink. His face was flushed from more than just the heat of the bar. His eyes took a few moments to focus on the note. He saw an address which made him smile. He read out a loud and then his face fell a little.

'What's wrong Joe?' asked Cooper. 'I'm sure it's pucker. You'll have to pay them. I don't want to mess this guy around.

'Keep your hair on. Nobody'll be messed around. It's just that it's a bit of a trip. I don't have a motor. Needs thinking about, that's all.'

He stared at the address a little bit more. His Billy was at this house, but now that he had an address, something that he'd gone out of his way to acquire it did present a problem. It was one thing to want to be near his child but what exactly was his plan. Suze had not been a consideration throughout all of this. Yet now it was becoming clear to him that his range of options was limited. What exactly was he proposing to do?

Kidnapping the child was out. That would create a nationwide uproar. It would mean prison, almost certainly. Suze would never agree to allowing Billy out of her sight. Besides which, he had not contributed a penny to his upkeep. How could he? Yet, the question could be levelled in a different way using the same words. How could he? It's not like he was so flush with money that he could afford to contribute to his upbringing never mind him and Suze.

No, it needed thinking about. How much did it cost to have a kid? It's not like it needed that much. Food. Clothes. He'd be going to school soon, so they'd feed him anyway.

The only problem was Suze.

There was no point in threatening her. That would only make thing worse. She would never agree to allow him to see the boy, at least without her being there too. That was about as likely as Pope becoming a Protestant.

Something had to be done about Suze. The problem was only one thing occurred to him. Again. It was a recurring thought that nagged at him like she used to do. He recoiled at the thought of it. There had to be another way.

'What's wrong, Joe?' asked Cooper. He had a smile on his face that Sanders did not like.

'What do you mean what's wrong?'

'You're not thinking of giving up are you?' pressed Cooper. He was enjoying his friend's discomfort.

'Of course not,' snapped Sanders. 'Just needs thinking bout.'

'You've had weeks to think about mate. It's time for action f you ask me.'

'No one's asking you,' replied Sanders sharply. His eyes ere blazing now. He was angry at Cooper but also at himself. Cooper was right. He'd had plenty of time to think about this nd he hadn't. In fact from the moment he'd asked his friend o speak to the copper he'd not given his boy much thought. He liked the idea of having his son around more than the ark, cold reality of what that would mean for him and his life, uch as it was.

Cooper did not look happy and turned to go but Sanders eached out and grabbed his arm. He rose from his seat and id, 'Here, don't go. What are you having?'

'Half a mild,' replied Cooper, slightly mollified by the hange in tone from Sanders. He sat down while Sanders went o the bar. He returned a minute later with two half pints.

'Look,' said Sanders. 'There's a lot to this.' For the next few inutes he laid out what was on his mind to his friend. Barry Cooper listened intently. He was not the brightest of men, but e was a loyal friend. His usefulness as a pal was principally in is physical presence. He was as tall as a tree and just bright. anders liked him. Cooper liked Sanders. They complimented ne another and often had been employed by the businessmen anders associated with as a pair.

How far was he prepared to go? All roads may lead to ome he thought but at that moment they led somewhere else, d he didn't like the thought of it. Not one bit. Yet, what else was there to be done. He sensed Cooper's eyes boring into him.

'Leave it with me Gary.'

*

It always seemed to rain when Jellicoe visited a cemetery. He wanted to ignore the idea of the sky weeping. It seemed too literary, too aware of itself. He walked towards the grave, each step heavier and heavier. Uncertainty gripped him. Was it guilt? This thought had never really left him: he was responsible. Had he acted in a different way it would not have happened. Something might have changed. Yet equally, he knew the chords of life vibrated as much to the playing of others as our own strumming. Who could really say if we are responsible for bad things never mind good? Things happen. They happen for a thousand and one reasons that are out of our control.

He was standing by the grave now, clutching the sodden flowers. He edged forward nervously and laid them down gently. Now he was unsure what to do. His mother, had she been there, would have insisted on the Rosary. This was meant to be a meditative prayer, but all Jellicoe could remember when they had said it as a family was bursting into laughter swiftly followed by his mother. The family that prays together stays together, she always said.

As he thought this, tears welled up in his eyes. The grave stared back at him unforgivingly. Water dripped from the rim of his hat, and he felt the damp seeping through his raincoat. A hand on his shoulder. He turned around to see his father.

'Come on son. You'll miss your train.'

Jellicoe nodded and they walked towards the car. His mother sat in the front passenger seat. She looked at her son a

214

he climbed into the car. They drove twenty minutes to the train station mostly in silence.

As Jellicoe got out of the car his father took his suitcase from the boot. They shook hands as they had done at the airport on a few weeks previously.

'For what it's worth son, you should stop blaming yourself. You must see that it wasn't your fault.'

Several hours later, Jellicoe was back in this flat alone with his cat. Monk was content to sit on his lap as the pair listened to the rain beat relentlessly against the window outside. Neither wanted to change their seat but Jellicoe knew that he had one visit to make. He stared at the bouquet of flowers wrapped in brown paper, sitting in the sink in the kitchen.

'Sorry old boy,' said Jellicoe, patting the black cat. 'I have to go.' Monk looked up at him with what was probably the cat equivalent of a roll of the eyes. Just when he was getting comfortable, too. 'I won't be away long,' added Jellicoe reading the expression on his cat's face.

Outside the flat, the light was dimming. The long nights were dropping hints of their imminent arrival. They would bring the usual increase in crime. Jellicoe, like many policemen, hated winter for reasons that went beyond a prejudice about stomping around streets in wind and rain.

He drove ten minutes, through the town to a suburb of the town with identical detached houses stretching out along an endless street. The front lawns were manicured, and every second garden seemed to have a rhododendron bush. Jellicoe glanced down at the flowers thinking they were not only somewhat obsolete but rather inadequate too when compared with the Versailles-like magnificence on display around him.

The house he was visiting was no different from all of the others on the road. Built in the thirties, it was two storeys high with black and white mock Tudor trimmings surrounded by a sea of red brick.

Jellicoe parked his car in the driveway. He hopped out of the car and walked slowly to the door clutching the flowers like the peace offering it was. The bell rang with a crisp, clear sound that was probably audible in Basingstoke. As he waited he realised his heart was beginning to race.

Was this guilt? Of course it was. It was the inescapable knowledge that he was responsible for what had happened. It never seemed to leave him. First with Sylvia and now with Burnett. Through the frosted glass in the door he saw a woman appear.

The door opened and it took her a few moments to recognise who it was. Rage flared in her eyes. It was an anger that was never very far away at the best of times, according to her husband who normally accompanied this comment with a rueful shake of the head.

'It's you,' said Mrs Elsie Burnett, the wife of Chief Inspector Reg Burnett. She was a woman in her late fifties stern of countenance, sturdy of build and strong of character. Too strong Clarkey would say. He, too, would accompany this comment with a rueful shake of the head.

Jellicoe thrust the flowers forward. She narrowly avoided 'tutting', but it was there on the pinched expression of contempt on her face as if someone had just broken wind next to her. However, she was English. This was a guest no matter how unwelcome. She reluctantly accepted the flowers and said 'You better come in.'

It wasn't quite 'Lovely to see you' but for the moment it was sufficient to cause a wave of relief to surge through Jellicoe. the worst was over. She hadn't thrown the flowers in his face.

'Go on through,' said Mrs Burnett.

Jellicoe walked towards a door he knew to be the living room. The television was on. He opened the door but did not walk in. Instead, he stood in the doorway regarded the man sitting on the sofa with his legs on a footstool. Stiped pyjamas peeked out from under his tartan dressing gown.

'Hello Chief,' said Jellicoe.

Burnett looked up and smile split his face, 'Well look who it is. Lord Peter Wimsey is gracing us with his presence.' Burnett followed this up by touching his forelock.

'I should have left you there,' said Jellicoe wandering over and sitting beside his boss.

'You wouldn't get my job, son, if that's what you're after. It would be Davies.'

'I don't want your job,' observed Jellicoe.

'Just as well,' replied Burnett. 'Reach me over my pipe.'

'Don't you dare,' said a voice from the doorway. Jellicoe lecided, wisely, to obey Mrs Burnett. 'I'll get you a tea. White vithout?' Jellicoe nodded meekly like he was being given an nstruction. 'When I get back I want to know what happened. 've stopped believing a word he ever tells me.'

After she disappeared, the two men waited a few moments until they heard sounds coming from the kitchen, then Jellicoe whispered to the chief, 'How are things?'

'You should have left me there,' replied Burnett with a roll of the eyes. 'She says she returned to the house two days later o find me gone. I think I just missed her when I left for ondon. Anyway, she's back now. Not a word of apology either. She says it was a wakeup call, for me mark you, to stop taking her for granted. For granted? What about me?'

The last remark was mouthed rather than stated as they heard the heavy tread of Mrs Burnett's slippered feet. She entered the room carrying a tray with a cup of tea and a jam sandwich.

'I didn't know if you'd eaten or not,' she said with all of the joie de vivre of a dentist informing a patient that an extraction will be necessary. Jellicoe accepted the tray with a show of the unctuous gratitude that was probably necessary at that moment.

'Now tell me what happened,' demanded Mrs Burnett. 'And how on earth did he get those burns around his wrists.'

'The handcuffs?' said Jellicoe without meaning to causing Burnett to choke on his tea. Jellicoe's eyes widened and he turned to Burnett who was turning puce in a combination of anger and no little panic.

'Handcuffs?' expostulated Mrs Burnett.

Jellicoe's eyes fell on a small film clapperboard. It was cracked with a hole in the middle of it. There was no question its presence in his pocket had probably saved Burnett's life HIs mind raced quickly and then inspiration struck.

'Restraints,' replied Jellicoe, recovering some composure and now beginning to enjoy himself. He glanced at Burnett who's eyes had narrowed to malevolent slits. There was a message in those eyes and that message was 'Tread carefully son'.

'Yes, restraints. After the ambulance collected him they had to tie his hands to the stretcher. I don't know if you have ever driven in Italy, Mrs Burnett, but Italians drive rather fast.'

'Bloody maniacs,' muttered Burnett.

'Anyway, what with stab wound, the loss of blood. The last thing they needed was for him to slide off the stretcher while they were driving to the hospital,' said Jellicoe. He was now working hard to suppress his laughter. The last trace of guilt that he'd felt for having nearly been the unwitting cause of Burnett's demise was slowly leaving him.

'Bloody Keystone Cops,' commented Mrs Burnett.

27

Jellicoe entered the detectives' room at the police station, and it seemed to him the man at the piano stopped playing and the saloon stopped talking. Superintendent Frankie was in Burnett's office with Detective Inspector, now acting Chief Inspector, Ivor Davies. Frankie and Davies looked up at Jellicoe's arrival. Frankie made a sign with his finger. He was gesturing towards the heavens or, in this case, the offices upstairs where he and Chief Constable Laurence Leighton sometimes resided. Jellicoe expected that the meeting he was about to join would be far from a trip to paradise if Frankie's pursed lips were any guide.

Frankie was out of the office in a flash with a terse, 'Come with me.'

Jellicoe said, 'yes sir,' and followed him. He risked a quick look to Detective Sergeant Yates and Detective Constable Wallace. Yates was making a motion with his hand that suggested he was about to be caned in the backside. Wallace was holding his nose and trying not to laugh.

Detective Sergeant Fogg entered just at that moment. He clocked Frankie's expression and then looked at Jellicoe. He too, supressed a smirk. Jellicoe and Frankie walked up the stairs in silence. Out on the third floor they entered a large outer office where the ever-fragrant beauty of Elodie Lumsden was busily typing a letter. She glanced at the expression on Frankie's face and then looked sympathetically at Jellicoe.

This was definitely not good.

The two men entered the office.

'Close the door,' snarled Frankie at Jellicoe even though it was perfectly plain that he was doing this anyway. 'Sit down.'

Frankie remained standing. It was an old trick. It worked if you were a large man. Frankie, rather like the Chief Constable, was a large man. He opened his legs shoulder width apart and leaned over pressing his two hands down on the table. The colour of his hands was a mixture of red on the fingers and white around the knuckles. From such an angle, Jellicoe judged he would be able to get the best purchase on the bawling out that the Superintendent was about to administer.

Frankie's face was red with anger even before he roared, 'Just what the hell were you playing at?'

*

In the outer office, much to Elodie Lumsden's surprise, the door burst open, and half a dozen men came spilling in led by DI Fogg. He was followed by Wallace, Yates, Constables Clarke and Wilkins. Fogg put his fingers to his mouth in a hushing motion to the rather alarmed half English, half French secretary. The last person to arrive was Winnie Leighton. Elodie wondered if there was anyone actually manning the front desk but then she noticed that 'Crumbs' Crombie was not there. He'd obviously drawn the short straw.

In fact, he had.

'Call down to the front desk,' whispered Clarke. 'Ol' Crumbs' wants to listen in.'

*

Inside the office, Superintendent Frankie's roar had only been the quiet before the storm. Impressively and much to Jellicoe's amazement the storm grew louder, angrier, and more threatening. It was had reached the point where Frankie was asking questions but not expecting an answer. To call them rhetorical would have been to overlay a gravitas that they were never meant to bear.

'Give me one bloody reason why I should not have you court martialled?'

Well, we're not in the army, thought Jellicoe but wisely demurred from offering this as a response. As it happened, Frankie had realised himself that this was perhaps the wrong service, so he quickly tacked in another direction before the words 'dishonourable discharge' were uttered.

'You're gross misconduct has reached the very highest levels and made fools of Chief Constable Leighton and me. You have unquestionably undermined the position of your own father. You have damn near caused a diplomatic incident with an important ally in Europe and worst of all, you came with a hair's breadth of causing the death of Chief Inspector Burnett.'

Frankie paused for a moment as he appeared to be winding himself up for one last push to the summit of what his voice could deliver in volume, rage and righteous indignation.

'Were it not for the fact that we are so badly under resourced I would have you walking the beat again son and make no mistake we have discussed this. We can't suspend you just so you can have another holiday and don't even think of resigning. You bloody owe us, son.'

Frankie jabbed his finger inches away from Jellicoe's nose. It took all of Jellicoe's resolve not to didge the mitt flying towards him.

'Chief Constable Leighton and I, in consultation with the Assistant Chief Constable of the Met, yes son, that's right, your father, have agreed the following action. You will not be dismissed but you will be demoted. As of this meeting you are hereby demoted to Detective Sergeant. This will be your rank until such time as we decide we will promote you and take it from me, son, that will be a bloody long time away. This will apply to any police station that you go to in case you take it in your head to flounce off. Again. In addition to losing rank, you will also take a Detective Sergeant's pay and benefits. Yes son, this is going to hurt.'

Jellicoe thought about the inheritance once more. Yes, he thought with some sadness, it was going to hurt, but Frankie had not quite finished yet.

'Detective Sergeant Fogg will now take your place as Detective Inspector.'

Now that really did hurt.

Outside in the outer office, Fogg greeted this news with a clenched fist and a grin. This disappeared when he saw the reaction of Wallace, Yates and Clarke. He shrugged and whispered, 'It's his own bloody fault. No point in blaming me.'

'Now get the hell out if this office, Jellicoe,' screamed Frankie, his eyes popping in an alarming way, coating Jellicoe in a spray of spittle.

Jellicoe rose from his seat and went to the door. He opened and went into the outer office. As he did so he heard the sound of the outer office door closing and footfalls outside. He frowned at the office which was empty save for Elodie Lumsden whose eyes were fixed on the paper in the typewriter.

Jellicoe wandered down the corridor with an overwhelming feeling of relief. It could have been so much worse. If Frankie had dismissed him he could have had no cause for complaint. There was no question that his father had pulled strings to ensure there was no inquiry. Perhaps the Met, a little battered and bruised following the inquest on Sylvia did not want to risk more bad publicity by disciplining him. A part of him, a part that he recognised as vanity, asked how could they? Thanks to his efforts, the case on Sylvia and Shirley Kenyon's killer was all but closed.

The Italian police had probably already confirmed that Silvio Riva, the proprietor of the weekly scandal magazine Realita! had led a double life. That Realita!, far from being the wellspring of justice was, in fact, a front to launder money from drugs, extortion, vice and all manner of criminal revenue while at the same time being a vehicle with which to blackmail Italian politicians from local to national level. The genius of the operation, and it was genius in Jellicoe's book, was all too clear Organised crime would bribe politicians and then forward the information to Realita! who would then threaten those that had been bribed. Every so often a sacrificial lamb would be found just to keep Realita's credibility and threat intact.

According to Commisario Conti, who Jellicoe was now in regular contact with, the rumour mill was suggesting, but there was no proof, that Realita was the brainchild of 'Lucky' Luciano himself. Of course proving this was another matter Luciano had remained under constant surveillance since his arrival in Italy a decade previously. His occasional arrests had been short-lived and resulted in humiliating climbdowns. Con remained optimistic that something in the extensive files of Realita! might link him to the Italian American mobster.

Jellicoe probably owed Conti a great debt. He had no doubt that despite their rather shaky beginning, Conti's regard for him had grown. He would have spoken up in Jellicoe's defence and pointed out that it was the Englishman who had made the breakthrough on linking Silvio Riva to organised crime. Previously this would have been unthinkable.

Jellicoe's mind turned to Silvio Riva. Il Cacciatore. The Hunter. The man who had almost killed his boss and, he realised, his friend, Chief Inspector Burnett. A magazine proprietor yet also a sicaro, a hitman. For nearly a decade he had successfully carried out dozens of murders at the behest of organised crime and not once had the gaze of suspicion been cast in his direction. It was astonishing to think that such a man could exist and operate with impunity for so long, but only one thing was more astonishing to Jellicoe than this. Silvio Riva was not alone. There was a second sicaro. A man who had saved the life of Jellicoe and who now had disappeared into the shadows once more.

It was impossible to be certain who the man was, but Jellicoe had his suspicions. One thing, though, was absolutely certain. Claudia had commissioned him to do exactly what he had done. Kill the other hitman. Jellicoe had no doubt Claudia had used him to draw out the other hitman. While Jellicoe and Burnett were the bait, the other man would wait, also like a hunter, to see who would come, and then kill them.

Jellicoe smiled as he thought of Claudia. A bereaved mother out for revenge and boy had she extracted an almighty retribution on those who had robbed her of her daughter and, by extension, her husband. She had disappeared now. He wondered idly where she was now.

He arrived down to the detectives' room. All the men were there, suspiciously busy working on their paperwork. Jellicoe grinned at them.

'I take it you heard every word.'

The room erupted into laughter. In a moment everyone was on their feet in order to shake hands with him. Fogg came over to him, hand outstretched, with a rueful grin.

'I suppose I should call you sir, now,' said Jellicoe.

'Damn right, son,' replied Fogg before bursting out onto that smoker's laugh, part deep chuckle, part cough.

Jellicoe turned to Wallace who was grinning with all of the enthusiasm of a Labrador puppy. He shook Jellicoe's hand.

'Glad to have you back, sir.'

'David,' said Jellicoe. 'I need a small favour from you. It may not be easy, so it'll require all your charm.'

'Yes?' asked Wallace, a smile of suspicion on his face.

'I need you to find a young woman for me. Her name is Susan...'

28

Three weeks earlier:

Cinecittà, Rome: 22nd August 1959

Culver Wendell had seen his friend Dino running towards a group of partygoers. This was a surprise to him. He hadn't realised Dino would be moonlighting at the film studio. The initial wonder of this had given way as the shocking realisation of what his friend was shouting registered with him. He was calling for a doctor; someone had been stabbed.

Culver tied Marilyn to a heavy nautical spotlight. She wouldn't be able to move it, even if she were so inclined. He ran in the direction that Dino had just come from, past the end of the recreated Via Veneto towards the smaller interior sets. He reasoned that if a doctor were needed then it would have been apparent with the reaction of the groups of people who were congregated in each interior, but they all seemed to be enjoying themselves. He sprinted towards the other side of the lot which was darker with all manner of equipment and pieces of scenery. From time to time he found himself hurdling over men and women lying on the ground.

It had been a while since Culver had demanded so much from a frame that had enjoyed a little bit too much pasta over his years in Italy. He was on the wrong side of burly and he was feeling it. His heart was pumping like a piston in a racing car.

And then he saw it.

Nick Jellicoe was standing in front of a man holding a pistol on him, but that man was suddenly assaulted by another who was holding a knife. The other man picked up the gun and pointed it at Jellicoe just as the music ceased. He wouldn't shoot without the music. Too risky. They were partially obscured by scenery so no one could see them.

Culver ducked behind a large wardrobe. He felt inside his pocket then took out a gun. If the sicaro could not shoot then nor could he. Too many questions would be asked.

So he waited.

Why was it taking so long. Jellicoe and the hitman seemed to be talking. He wished he could see the face of the man, but he was turned away. Not that it mattered. What was one more death? At least this man had it coming. Culver wondered if this was this was the other sicaro. The man he knew as Il Cacciatore.

He'd never really thought of the man standing by Jellicoe as a rival. As far as Culver was concerned, they were in the same business, but it wasn't as if they were in competition. If anything, the other man had cultivated his 'hunter' image by mostly using a knife. For Culver it was less about method and all about the outcome. How many ways had he used to kill? A dozen perhaps but he counted machine guns, pistols and rifles as different weapons because each had its own characteristics. Oddly, he'd never used a knife. Perhaps this was a professional courtesy, or perhaps he'd never fancied the idea of close quarters. This was not because he lacked courage. Just too much risk. He was a low-risk kind of guy.

Then he would get to write the obituary. This always gave him a kick. It had a nice symmetry to it, he thought. Who'd have thought it, an obituary writer who moonlights as a killer. As covers went, it was close to genius in Culver's view. Talk about hiding in plain sight.

He was aiming his pistol now.

Then the music started masking the sound of his shot.

He watched Il Cacciatore crumple to the ground. Then he ducked behind the scenery and ran back to Marilyn. Quickly he unhooked the bulldog's lead from the light and began to retrace his footsteps towards Jellicoe and the man he'd shot.

He passed people who were still dancing or drinking or indulging in activity that would have them arrested in any other public situation. All were oblivious to the drama taking a matter of feet away.

He passed a clapperboard that read: La Dolce Vita. Underneath, someone had written in chalk, 'e finito'. It's over. □

29

Three weeks later:

Milan, Pinacoteca di Brera, Italy: 9th September 1959

Claudia Temple sat down at a bar in the centre of Milan just outside her favourite art museum in the city. She savoured the dark brick buildings around her, the sight and sound of her fellow countrymen shouting, laughing and gesticulating wildly as only Italians could. It was good to be back.

Her hair was now honey blonde and she wore sunglasses like a movie star. Men on the street cast surreptitious looks her way. She ignored them. Instead, she sipped a café lungo and opened the newspaper, Corriere d'Informazione. A smile crossed her face as she re-read for fifth time the obituary that featured in the newspaper. It was written by Culver Wendell. She savoured the exquisite irony of the copy.

Obituary: Silvio Riva

The memorial service has taken place to celebrate the life of magazine owner, Silvio Riva following his death on a film lot at Cinecittà three weeks ago. His death was greeted with shock among the community of Italian journalists and led to half day walk out in protest at the ongoing threat to free speech posed by organised crime

Silvio Riva was born on the island of Sicily in 1928. He early life was spent on the island with his family in the town of Carini. Despite his subsequent career and success firstly as a journalist and then as a magazine proprietor, Riva actually left school at the age of sixteen to work in his father's business. Roggero Riva was a butcher in the town which is a few kilometres from Palermo.

Following the death of his father at the hands of unknown mafioso, young Silvio took up the family trade of butchery and made quite a success of his profession. However, his ambitions lay beyond the island. Little is known of his life between the ages of twenty-six and thirty-one. Friends say that he spoke little of his activities in this period, but we do know that he ended up writing for a newspaper in Milan from 1953 to 1955. Ironically, given his recent demise, his reports covered the activities of organised crime in northern Italy. They consistently drew glowing reviews from the public and the respect of his fellow journalists not to mention the forces of law and order.

Silvio Riva announced himself to the wider public in 1956 when he started up his own weekly magazine to feed the insatiable demand of the Italian public for fact-based stories related the blight that has afflicted this country for so long: organised crime. His magazine Realita! stood as a beacon of truth in the often grey, amorphous world where crime, politics, justice and power exist in a symbiotic relationship.

The world of journalism, even butchery, has lost a unique man; a man of singular talent, dedicated to slicing through the flesh of injustice and corruption in the unwavering pursuit of the cause that he valued most in this new, post-war Italy: the truth.

Commisario Fausto Conti confirms that the investigation into his violent death continues but they have no leads on who committed this attack not just on a man of such striking talents but on all of us who share his vision for an Italy where the cancer of crime is cut from the body politic.

Silvio Riva - Born, Sicily 12th March 1928 - Died, Rome xx August 1959

Claudia drained the rest of her coffee and set the newspaper down. She looked up into the blue sky. She wanted to fee happy, but she knew this was not possible. She wondered if she would ever feel happy again?

The answer was probably but not just yet. She had achieved some form of retribution on those that had taken everything away from her. It was not finished yet. It would never finish until she found a way to bring down Lentini and the De Luca family, but she had made a start. She'd hurt them. They would come after her, but they would have a job finding Claudia Temple. She died the day her husband had taken a gun to himself. She was free now. The rest of her life would be dedicated to this one cause. She rose from the table and gracefully manoeuvred her way onto the street to join the throng of Milanese going to work.

*

As Claudia Temple floated away from the bar outside the Pinacoteca di Brera, Felix M. Scheffler rose from his bed. He glanced down at the young woman lying asleep and hoped he would remember her name before she awoke. Lying on the bed was the same newspaper that Claudia Temple had been reading over a thousand kilometres away in Milan.

He padded over to the window and opened the shutters. The fact that he was somewhat unclothed did not cross his mind. An old woman looked up at him from the street and turned away in disgust. This made him smile. Old crone, he thought. He glanced back down at the young woman but no

232

inspiration as to her name was forthcoming. As long she was paid, he doubted it mattered.

He opened the window but did not linger. Instead, he went over to the phone by his bed. He sat down on the bed and picked up a notebook. He flicked through a few of the pages before finding the number that he needed. Then he dialled a number. He waited a few moments then he heard someone on the other end of the line. There was no greeting or 'how are you?'

'It's me. Have you read the obituary? Have you found his replacement?'

The voice at the other end of the line confirmed that he had.

'Ciao Lucky,' said Scheffler and hung up.

30

London, England, 14th Sept 1959

Joe Sanders was missing his beloved Hammers today. For once, though, it did not matter. He had family business to attend to. Long overdue family business. Barry Cooper was driving the car. A light rain was falling but this was enough to wreak havoc on their windscreen as one of the wipers was not working. The mood in the car as a result was febrile. Sanders on the one hand, was grateful for the lift. On the other, the bloody wiper was driving him nuts. It seemed to him there was a fair to even chance they would not make it to their final destination and all because his mate had not fixed the bloody wiper.

Sanders watched as a big lorry sped towards him. He gripped the seat and almost shut his eyes. Cooper, the oaf seemed to be enjoying himself. It was as if he was on a holiday a jaunt to the seaside. In some senses he was. He quite like Bognor. If it wasn't for helping out Joe he might have made weekend of it, but Joe was a bit moody. Perhaps he should have sorted out the wiper in retrospect. Too late now.

They had a job to do.

He glanced at Sanders just in time to see him wince as another lorry passed them. This made Cooper smile.

'Keep your bloody eyes on the road, will you?' exclaimed Sanders.

'Keep your hair on, mate. Nearly there.'

Nearly there, all right, but at what cost? The last couple of hours had taken years of his life, thought Sanders. A year he'd waited for this. A bloody year and when the times comes he's shaking like a schoolboy in front of the headmaster. He wanted to communicate power, assurance and intent. Instead, he was perspiring, nervous and jerking at every hint of threat.

'Number 27,' said Cooper, pointing to an unprepossessing door on an unprepossessing street of red brick terraced houses. Cooper began to sing, 'Oh I do like to be beside the sea side.'

'Leave it out, moron,' said Sanders. Cooper began to cackle at this which made Sanders, who was getting out of the car, smile too. The smile hid the fear he was feeling. He slammed the door shut a little more firmly than he'd intended. Cooper swore at him causing Sanders to raise his hand in a half-hearted mea culpa.

He walked to the door like a man heading to the gallows. Paint was peeling from the frame. A thin window strip down the middle allowed him to look inside. He saw distorted shapes moving around.

He looked at the rusted metal door knocker with some distaste. To think, his son living in this. It wasn't right. Something had to be done. He rapped the door three times, firmly but not so hard as to be threatening.

A figure dressed in cream, from what he could see, approached the door. It was a woman. Pretty large too by the looks of it, he thought. She opened the door slightly and peered out from the crack. There was little in her expression that suggested welcome.

'Yes?' she snapped. She clearly hated men, he thought.

'I've some to see Suze. Sorry, Susan Dillon. Is she here?'

'Who is it,' called a voice from inside.

'Suze, it's Joe,' called Sanders from the rain-specked pavement.

Silence.

'You're not wanted here,' said the woman and began to shut the door but Sanders had wedged his foot into prevent her. It hurt damnably.

Suze appeared in the corridor and saw what was happening. There was fear in her eyes.

'Suze, come on. Let me in,' appealed Sanders. 'I could bust this door down if I wanted to, you know I could.'

'Let him in Penny,' said Suze calmly.

Penny turned around with disapproval etched deeply into her face.

'You sure?'

She received a nod. Penny stood back and Sanders entered the house. Suze looked at him. he seemed to have lost weight but he was as sharply dressed as ever. Then she realised he was wearing the suit she'd sold him.

'It's your suit,' confirmed Sanders. There was a nervous smile on his face that did nothing for him, but she felt oddly reassured.

'Can I see him?' asked Sanders. The appeal was childlike. It was like he was begging.

Penny did not like what she was saying, and she was not woman to stay silent when disapproval could communicate forcefully.

236

'Suze don't let him. Don't trust him.'

'Please,' appealed Sanders. He remained standing at the doorway.

'Let him come though, Pen,' replied Suze. She turned away and walked through a door. Sanders followed her down to the door which led through to a small sitting room with an unlit gas fire. The room was cold. Suze was standing by another door in which he could see the foot of a bed. He approached the door, heart racing. Suze stood back and he went in.

It was a Queen-sized bed. One half of it was empty. In the other was a small child buried under the bed clothes.

'He's sleeping. Don't wake him,' said Suze.

Sanders went around the bed to the side where his son was sleeping. He knelt down and looked into his face. He'd changed so much over the last year. It was his son and no mistake. He had his hair and nose. A smile broke out over Sanders as he looked at the boy. Relief, too. He wanted so much to pick him up and hold him. He'd never wanted anything more.

'Joe,' said Suze.

Sanders looked up at Suze and nodded. He rose to his feet and walked around the bed. Back in the sitting room, they were alone.

'You shouldn't be here, Joe,' said Suze. She was twisting her hands in front of her. Sanders sensed that Penny was standing by the door.

Now was his moment.

*

David Wallace had come through for him as Jellicoe knew he would. He'd found the address of Susan Dillon. As Jellicoe drove into Bognor he wondered what favours he owed his source. Not his problem, though. This was how you played the game. Wallace would learn and use it when he was in a senior position for that was where he was most assuredly bound while he was heading in the opposite direction.

Jellicoe entered into the housing estate and saw endless rows of terraced houses. He drove slowly down the street counting down the numbers: thirty-three, thirty-one, twenty-nine and then he saw his destination. There was a car a parked outside it, so he slipped his car in behind.

A light smattering of rain greeted him as he climbed out into the open air. He pulled his collar up and walked past the car. Out of habit he cast his eyes down at the car. There was a man in the driver's seat. This seemed odd to him. For a moment he thought to pull out his warrant card and approach the car but stopped himself. Perhaps he needed to be less suspicious. Another thought occurred to him. He still had his old warrant card with his old rank. The new one still hadn't come through. He smiled at this, but it was a thin smile. Gallows humour.

Jellicoe rapped on the knocker and saw a large shape appear in the door window. She opened the door slightly and stared at Jellicoe in the manner of a woman who did not trust men and him, in particular.

'Good morning,' said Jellicoe deciding against attempting smile. 'My name is Jellicoe. I understand a Susan Dillon live here. I'm from the police.'

The woman's eyes widened. She stood back and opene the door.

'He's in there,' she said in a horrified whisper. Jellico frowned at this. He looked towards the door where the woma was pointing. It was opening.

238

This was the moment Saunders had been waiting for over a year. He wasn't going to let it pass. He let the energy build up inside him.

'Take me back Suze,' said Sanders. It was barely a whisper. He couldn't stop the tears that were now stinging his eyes.

'No Joe. I can't go back to that.'

'Please Suze. We can make this work.'

'We can't Joe,' insisted Suze. She shook her head and turned away.

'I made a mistake, Suze. I made a lot of mistakes, but I've changed. I will change. I want to be with him. With you.'

'No, Joe,' said Suze. She too had tears in her eyes. 'I can't have Billy growing up with a father who steals or deals or whatever it is you do. I can't have Billy living in a house where we don't know if his dad will come back and if he does what he'll be like.'

Sanders stood looking at Suze. There was nothing he could say. He could see that she was right. He felt a wave of defeat assail him. He couldn't look at her as she stared back at him, his hands by his side.

Sanders nodded. He wiped his eyes and then gazed back at Suze. There was nothing else he could say. He took a deep breath and said, 'I know Suze. I want to be a part of his life. I'll change Suze. I really will.'

'You should go now, Joe.'

Sanders nodded once more and walked towards the door. Someone was rapping on the door outside. When he reached the door he turned to the mother of his boy.

'If I write to you will you send me a picture of him? Of you both?'

Suze was silent for a moment and then she nodded. Sanders smiled; he opened the door of the room. As he stepped into the corridor he saw a man walking down the corridor.

Penny said, 'Suze, this man's from the police.' This was more a warning to Sanders than information for her friend.

'It's all right, Pen. Joe's just going,' said Suze. There was no fear in her voice now.

Jellicoe watched the red-rimmed eyes of the man called Joe walk towards him. The two men nodded to one another and then Sanders was out the front door. Jellicoe had a good memory for men who operated on the other side of the law. He didn't recognise Sanders, but he could not stop himself wondering about the warning by the woman who had let him in.

Sanders, meanwhile, was fighting to control the emotions raging within him. The sight of his son, Suze also, had awoken feelings that were so much stronger than he had hitherto experienced; he could barely breathe. He reached the car and almost fell into the passenger seat.

'What happened?' demanded Cooper. 'Where's the boy?' He hadn't driven two or more hours down to the coast only to return empty-handed. Sanders said nothing, still fighting a war he'd never expected to fight, and which life had ill-prepared him for. 'Joe, are you listening? Where's Billy?'

'With his mother,' snarled Sanders.

Cooper could not believe what he was hearing. He glared at his friend. Sanders could see the anger in his eyes.

'Are you having me on?' shouted Cooper. 'Are you telling me we drove all the way down here for that?'

240

Sanders glared back at him. 'What's it to you?' he shouted back. Cooper was not having it, not by a long chalk. He opened the car door. 'Where are you going?' demanded Sanders, getting out of the car also.

Cooper was half-way to the house now, he spun around and pointed at Sanders. 'I'll tell you where I'm bloody going, Joe. I'm going in there to do what you should have done and get your nipper,' he shouted.

'No,' said Sanders, holding his gaze steady on his big friend.

'What do you mean no?' scowled Cooper, walking menacingly towards his friend.

'I mean no. Not like this,' said Sanders. His voice had quietened down. Cooper stared at his friend with incredulity. Sanders was getting back in the car. 'Let's go Joe.'

Cooper glared at Sanders and exhaled noisily. He shook his head and returned to the car.

'Not like this, Joe,' repeated Sanders, as Cooper landed heavily on the front seat.

*

Jellicoe looked at Suze and he saw a flash of recognition in her eyes.

'You're that copper,' she said.

This made Jellicoe smile and he nodded. He gestured towards the man who had passed him.

'Was that the father of your boy?'

Suze nodded. She turned and walked into the room. Jellicoe assumed she meant for him to follow her, so he did. They sat down. Jellicoe looked around the room. It was small, a little cold but it was tidy. Through another door he saw there was a bed. Suze noticed where he was looking and smiled. 'Billy's asleep. He's a sleeper, that one,' she said proudly.

Jellicoe glanced at his watch. It was just after nine in the morning. He'd been up since before six.

'Clearly,' agreed Jellicoe who had no idea of this was a good or bad thing. He noticed Penny was standing by the door. He turned to her and said, 'You can join us. I think this concerns you too. By the way, I don't know how the father would have found you. I'll need to look into that. Is he giving you trouble?'

Suze glanced at Penny but then shook her head firmly. She said, 'No. There's going to be no trouble from him.'

Jellicoe nodded doubtfully. He would check anyway. However, he judged from what he'd seen that the father was not a threat. He'd looked beaten. A dull acceptance of how things were, but he would check anyway.

'I never had a chance to say thank you for coming forward like you did. It took courage, Susan. You saved my career. We caught the man who...' Jellicoe stopped for a moment. He couldn't form the words. His throat tightened and all at once he found it difficult to breathe.

'There's something I wanted to tell you. A decision I made a week or two ago that affects you and ladies like you.'

242

31

A few hours later:

'I'm begging you, Nick. Look I'm on my hands and knees my friend. Don't do it.'

Nick Jellicoe held the telephone away from him then put the receiver back to his ear and said, 'Firstly Taranjit, you may have noticed that we're talking on a telephone, and I can't see you. Secondly, it's too late. The deed is done. I have given the money away. It's gone. All of it.'

Taranjit all but howled at the other end of the line.

'Why Nick? Why didn't you speak to me? We could have done something.'

'No, Taranjit,' confirmed Jellicoe. 'I could not live with myself knowing the source of this money.'

'You don't know that for certain.'

'I do,' said Jellicoe firmly. 'Anyway, you had to see where she was living. The hopelessness of it all. I want more women like her to have a secure place where they can go to.'

'You said that she may go back to him, though. How do you square that with your bleeding-heart conscience?'

'She may or may not go back. He sounds like a bad lot, but he looked pretty cut up about seeing the boy. Who knows? The bigger point is that the money is almost certainly dirty.

Drugs money. I can't live on the proceeds of crime, Taranjit. You must see that.' This was greeted by a silence at the other end of the line which suggested that the lawyer could entirely see how a man could live on a small fortune free of financial worry for the rest of his life.

Then Jellicoe added, 'I've sent you a cheque for the money I owe you. It came from the inheritance, so you'll be glad to hear that my conscience isn't entirely without blemish.'

As he said this he looked at the dry-cleaned Brioni two suits lying on his coffee table. No, he was not completely lacking a pragmatic streak. This had even extended to paying in advance the rent of his flat for another twelve months.

'Well I'm very disappointed in you young man,' scolded Taranjit but he didn't sound it and Jellicoe was profoundly unworried. The call ended soon after. Jellicoe went over to his record player and put on his recent acquisition, 'Kind of Blue' by Miles Davis. It had come out whilst he was in Rome and was quite the best piece of jazz music Jellicoe had ever heard. He let the cool, romantic, melancholic melodies wash over him.

At some point during 'Flamenco Sketches' Monk hopped up onto his knee. This usually meant that he was settling down for a nap or he wanted to be fed. As the cat had just woken up Jellicoe suspected it was the latter. He rose from the seat and carried Monk with him.

With a free hand he opened a cupboard in the kitchen.

'Well Monk, old boy, you have a choice of Whiskas, Whiskas or, is that a Whiskas I see peeking out from behind the other tins of Whiskas?'

Monk offered no opinion either way so Jellicoe selected the first tin he could find and emptied a good proportion of the contents into a bowl and placed it on the floor.

With a heavy heart he stood up again and looked back at the cupboard. After a couple of weeks dining in the best restaurants in Rome he faced a starker choice on the culinary front. A few tins of Heinz Beans stared back at him dolefully. With a sigh he lifted one down and pulled a tin opener out from an open drawer.

La dolce vita, insofar as it had ever existed, was over. Life was returning to normal.

The End

About the Author

Jack Murray was born in Northern Ireland but has spent over half his life living just outside London, except for some periods spent in Australia, Monte Carlo, and the US.

An artist, as well as a writer, Jack's work features in collections around the world and he has exhibited in Britain, Ireland, and Monte Carlo.

There are now seven books in the Kit Aston series.

A spin off series from the Kit Aston novels was published in 2020 featuring Aunt Agatha as a young woman solving mysterious murders.

Jack has just finished work on a World War II trilogy. The three books look at the war from both the British and the German side. Jack has just signed with Lume Books who will now publish the war trilogy. The three books will all have been published by end October 2022.

Acknowledgements

It is not possible to write a book on your own. There are contributions from so many people either directly or indirectly over many years. Listing them all would be an impossible task.

Special mention therefore should be made to my wife and family who have been patient and put up with my occasional grumpiness when working on this project.

My brother, Edward, has helped in proofing and made supportive comments that helped me tremendously. Thank you, too, to Debra Cox who has been a wonderful help on reducing the number of irritating errors that have affected my earlier novels. A word of thanks to Charles Gray and Brian Rice who have provided legal and accounting support.

My late father and mother both loved books. They encouraged a love of reading in me. In particular, they liked detective books, so I must tip my hat to the two greatest writers of this genre, Sir Arthur and Dame Agatha.

Following writing, comes the business of marketing. My thanks to Mark Hodgson and Sophia Kyriacou for their advice in this important area. Additionally, a shout out to the wonderful folk on 20Booksto50k.

Finally, my thanks to the teachers who taught and nurtured a love of writing.

This is a work of fiction. However, it references real-life individuals. Gore Vidal, in his introduction to Lincoln, writes that placing history in fiction or fiction in history has been unfashionable since Tolstoy and that the result can be accused of being neither. He defends the practice, pointing out that writers from Aeschylus to Shakespeare to Tolstoy have done so with not inconsiderable success and merit.

I have mentioned a number of key real-life individuals and events in this novel. My intention, in the following section, is to explain a little more about their connection to this period and this story. I have been greatly helped in my research by the following books which are well worth reading to understand better this fascinating period in Italy's post war history – Dolce Vita Confidential by Shawn Levy, Death and the Dolce Vita by Stephen Gundle.

La Dolce Vita (1960)

Written and directed by Federico Fellini, *La Dolce Vita* is one of the greatest film ever made. The film ranked 10th in BBC's 2018 list of The 100 greatest foreign language films voted by 209 film critics from 43 countries around the world. Why is this?

Made during 1959, even before it was released it was attracting controversy in Italy for its subject matter and the light it cast over the decadent lifestyle of the rich and famous who inhabited the café society of Rome's Via Veneto. The dark underbelly of this world is hinted at often in the film, the fish motif is believed to reference the death of Wilma Montesi a few years previously. The film also referenced other true events such as the 'orgy' involving the Turkish model Aiche Nana the previous year at Rugantino. As soon as the Vatican condemned the film, its success was sealed. It was a global sensation and garnered several Academy Award nominations and one statuette for costume as well as carrying off the Palme D'Or at Cannes.

Unlike many popular and critically acclaimed films, its influence lives on even today in that it made famous the swarms of photographers that flock around celebrities and gave them their name (after one of the character's in the film) – paparazzi. And many images from the film remain eternal like the city that gave birth to the film – Anita Eckberg in the fountain, the enormous monster fish on the beach.

ADD
Mina

Victor Ciufa

The Montesi Case (1953-60)
Wilma Montesi was a twenty-one-year woman whose body was found on a beach near Rome. For the next six years the

unsolved murder was the subject of intense speculation among public and media alike. The speculation centred on the involvement of this quiet, Catholic virgin girl with the most politicians, artists and criminal gang leaders. The case has never been satisfactorily solved. It was a defining moment in post-war Italy as it revealed that despite the end of Fascist rule in the country, the rich and powerful elite remained immune from prosecution.

Federico Fellini (1920 – 93)

Federico Fellini was one of a group of Italian film makers who effectively came to define the language of world cinema along with Vittorio di Sica (The Bicycle Thieves) , Roberto Rossellini (Rome, Open City) and Luchino Visconti (The Leopard). A multi-Academy Award winner, Fellini's most film is *La Dolce Vita.*

Paparazzi

Named after the character Paparazzo in La Dolce Vita, the wolf pack of Italian photographers were a regular sight on Via Veneto during the late fifties and early sixties. The went from bar to bar snapping away at the rich and the famous. Their presence was not always welcome. The English actor Anthony Steel was famously photographed attacking them and his wife, Anita Eckberg, who was normally much less volatile eventuall found their intrusiveness too much. She was also snapped wit a real-life archer's bow and arrow. Soon the photographers found themselves under attack with arrows flying towards the The most famous of the group were Tazio Secchiaroli whose work often made it onto the scandal magazines such *Attualita* and Pierluigi Praturlon who originally snapped Anita Eckberg in the Trevi Fountain, giving birth to the idea that Fellini subsequently made famous.